Carol Marinelli recently filled in a form where she was asked for her job title and was thrilled, after all these years, to be able to put down her answer as 'writer'. Then it asked what Carol did for relaxation. After chewing her pen for a moment, Carol put down the truth—'writing'. The third question asked—'What are your hobbies?' Well, not wanting to look obsessed or, worse still, boring, she crossed the fingers on her free hand and answered 'swimming and tennis'. But, given that the chlorine in the pool does terrible things to her highlights, and the closest she's got to a tennis racket in the last couple of years is watching the Australian Open, I'm sure you can guess the real answer!

Recent books by Carol Marinelli:

Mills & Boon® Medical Romance™

SECRETS OF A CAREER GIRL††
DR DARK AND FAR TOO DELICIOUS††
NYC ANGELS: REDEEMING THE PLAYBOY**
SYDNEY HARBOUR HOSPITAL:
　AVA'S RE-AWAKENING*
HERS FOR ONE NIGHT ONLY?
CORT MASON—DR DELECTABLE
HER LITTLE SECRET
ST PIRAN'S: RESCUING PREGNANT CINDERELLA†
KNIGHT ON THE CHILDREN'S WARD

**NYC Angels
*Sydney Harbour Hospital
†St Piran's Hospital
††Secrets on the Emergency Wing

Mills & Boon® Modern™ Romance

A LEGACY OF SECRETS‡
PLAYING THE DUTIFUL WIFE
BEHOLDEN TO THE THRONE~
BANISHED TO THE HAREM~
AN INDECENT PROPOSITION
A SHAMEFUL CONSEQUENCE
HEART OF THE DESERT
THE DEVIL WEARS KOLOVSKY

~Empire of the Sands
‡Sicily's Coretti Dynasty

**These books are also available in eBook format
from www.millsandboon.co.uk**

With love to Fiona McArthur
I love our chats
C xxx

Praise for
Carol Marinelli:

'A heartwarming story about taking a chance and not
letting the past destroy the future. It is strengthened by
two engaging lead characters and a satisfying ending.'
—*RT Book Reviews* on
THE LAST KOLOVSKY PLAYBOY

'Carol Marinelli writes with sensitivity,
compassion and understanding, and
ST PIRAN'S: RESCUING PREGNANT CINDERELLA
is not just a powerful romance but an uplifting
and inspirational tale about starting over,
new beginnings and moving on.'
—*CataRomance*

If you love Carol Marinelli,
you'll fall head over heels
for Carol's sparkling, touching, witty debut.

PUTTING ALICE BACK TOGETHER

available from MIRA® Books

CHAPTER ONE

So it had been too good to be true!

Marnie Johnson drove slowly down Beach Road with a sense of mounting unease. The modern apartments and townhouses she had inspected just a couple of weeks ago were slowly giving way to dilapidated renovators' delights with sprawling, overgrown gardens. These were the type of homes that would require a whole lot of TLC for anyone to live comfortably in them—and the one thing Marnie didn't have was time to give a new home a lot of attention.

Almost certain that she had the job of nurse unit manager at the Bayside Hospital on Melbourne's Mornington Peninsula, Marnie had spent the afternoon after her interview looking at suitable homes to rent and had fallen in love with this street in particular. Yes, it was expensive but it was still a lot cheaper than her smart city apartment. She had been taken in by the sun-drenched, sparkling apartments with views that looked out over the bay and the townhouses with their balconies perfectly angled—just right for relaxing after a busy day, and Marnie certainly intended to be busy.

When the job offer had been confirmed Marnie had found herself far more stretched for time than usual, what with finishing up her old role and celebrating her sea change with friends. Yes, it had been a gamble but, after a lengthy conversation with Dave, the real estate agent who had shown her around, she had signed a month's lease on a house unseen, having been told that it was very similar to the ones she had inspected.

Similar!

The only similarity to the homes Marnie had been shown was that they each had a front door. Not that Marnie could see this particular one—it was obscured by overgrown bushes and trees, and the grass, as Marnie walked up the path, was waist high.

Never trust a real estate agent.

Marnie knew that but had been taken in when Dave had told her that this home had just come on the market and there were no photos yet. She had been so stretched that, for once, the very organised Marnie had taken her eye off the ball.

And look what happened when she did!

Pushing the door open, Marnie stepped inside and it was easily as bad as she had been expecting.

Marnie pulled out her phone and when the real estate agent's receptionist answered she asked to be put through to Dave. Marnie could hear the irritation coming through in her own voice—her usually lilting Irish accent was now sounding a touch brusque and harsh and she fought to check it.

'Dave is at an auction,' the receptionist that Marnie had collected the keys from explained. 'I'm not expecting him to come back to the office today, though I can call him and leave a message asking him to get in touch with you.'

Marnie bit back a smart response—after all, none of this was the young woman's fault. 'Yes, if you could ask him to call me as soon as possible, I'd appreciate it.'

There wasn't a hope that Dave would be calling back today, Marnie just knew it.

Tomorrow was Sunday and on Monday she started her new job and there simply wouldn't be time to arrange more inspections and shift her things again—she made sure that she led by example and she wasn't going to spend the first week in her new role trying to sort out somewhere else to live. She looked around at the grimy beige walls and told herself that once she had washed them down and cleaned the dusty windows, the place might not be so bad after all—though Marnie was sure she was fooling herself. As she wandered from room to room it grew increasingly hard to stay positive. The place didn't even have a bath—just a very mouldy-looking shower that would certainly need a good scrub before she used it. 'What is it with Australians and their showers?' Marnie asked herself out loud—she liked to have a bath in the evening to relax.

Letting out a sigh, she gave up dwelling on it—she'd been through far worse than this.

The removal truck would be arriving with her furniture at eight o'clock tomorrow, along with two of her brothers, Ronan and Brendan.

So she'd better get cleaning!

Marnie tied her thick black hair into a ponytail and headed out to her car to collect the bucket, bleach and vacuum cleaner that she had brought for the job, though she had expected it to be a far easier one. Still, if there was one thing Marnie excelled at it was organisation and cleaning. She'd have this place sorted in no time.

Men! Marnie thought as she lugged in the equipment. They took one look at her china-blue eyes and petite but curvy figure, saw her smiling face, heard her soft accent and thought that they had worked her out.

No one had ever worked her out!

Dave had no idea what he had let himself in for.

She took a call just as she was getting ready to start—it was Matthew, a friend that she went out with now and then.

'How's the new place?' Matthew asked.

'Grand!' Marnie lied. She certainly wasn't about to tell Matthew her mistake. He had thought she had gone a bit crazy when she had announced that she was leaving the city and moving out to the bayside suburb.

'You'll be back,' Matthew had warned. 'You'll soon be bored out of your mind.'

Marnie would like ten minutes to be bored, she thought as she chatted to him for a few moments and then ended the call.

It never entered her mind to ask him to come and help. Matthew was starting to get just a bit too familiar and Marnie didn't like that. She worked very hard at keeping all areas of her life separate. Family, work, social life—all were neatly separated, even her sex life. At thirty-one years old Marnie had long decided this was the way that worked best for her. She was an independent woman and certainly didn't want Matthew coming over to gloat about her real estate mistake and, worse, meet her brothers—that would render her relationship with Matthew far more than it was and Marnie had no intention of that happening.

Marnie opened every window throughout the house to let the sun stream in and then started her cleaning in the kitchen, gradually working her way outwards. She stopped occasionally for a drink and to admire her own handiwork. She was like a mini-tornado once she got going. Rubber gloves on, Marnie washed down the walls and cleaned the windows. The curtains she took down and hung out in the sun and, before putting them back, she vacuumed and mopped the floors, all the while thinking about Monday and the challenges that lay ahead.

She was looking forward to running a department. She had been an associate in a large city hospital for a few years but, realising her senior had no plans to leave and loathing having to answer to anyone, when she had seen the job at Bayside advertised she had taken the plunge. As she worked on, Marnie thought back to her interview. The place needed a strong leader, she had been told—and Marnie was certainly that. Christine, her predecessor, had apparently spent more time in the office than taking care of the department. The off-duty was a joke—the shifts dependent, it would seem, on who had brought Christine the most coffee. For now the place was being run by Cate Nicholls, who had chosen not to take the role permanently as she was soon to be married.

The emergency department was woefully short of doctors, though that, Marnie had been told, was being addressed and there were two new consultants starting soon. Another problem that had been hinted at was that one of the consultants, Harry Worthington, who hadn't been present at Marnie's interviews, was using the nursing staff as a babysitter to his twins.

'Not any more!' had been Marnie's swift response, and she had seen Lillian, the director of nursing, not only give a brief smile but write something on the notes in front of her.

It was then Marnie had known she had the job.

Harry Worthington!

As Lillian had shown her around the department Marnie had learnt a little bit more about the staffing issues and had found out that Harry was a recent widow and single father to four-year-old twins.

Marnie hadn't let on that the name was a familiar one but she had smothered a little smile when she'd thought of the once wild Harry now a consultant and single father.

Who would ever have thought it?

Ready now to tackle the shower, Marnie took down the shower curtain and soaked it with a good measure of bleach then stripped off into her underwear. As she started to scrub the grimy walls she thought about her early student nurse days. She had done the first year of training at Melbourne Central before, for personal reasons, transferring to the Royal to complete her training—it had been at Melbourne Central that their paths had loosely crossed. Loosely because, apart from 'What's his blood pressure doing?' or 'Can you get me his file?' Harry had never so much as spoken directly to her when she had been there, though she had felt the ripple effect when he'd entered the ward or canteen and she had heard an awful lot about him!

As a junior doctor, his wild ways, combined with very good looks, had assured that Harry had never lacked female attention. The mere whisper that Harry would be at a party in the doctors' mess would guarantee that the number of attendees swelled. Marnie had been head over heels with Craig, her first boyfriend, at the time. Living away from home, away from her strict parents and the responsibility of taking care of her younger brothers, Marnie had been too busy embracing her first taste of freedom to give Harry Worthington more than a moment's thought. But, a fair bit older and a whole lot wiser, kneeling back on her heels, Marnie thought about him now.

She remembered that he was tall and very long-limbed. His hair was brown and had always been superbly cut because no matter what the hour, be it nine a.m. and just starting or eight p.m. and just heading for home, it had always fallen into perfect shape. He had surely invented designer stubble and there had often been sniggers in the staff canteen when a nurse had appeared with Harry rash! He had worked hard, partied harder and completely lived up to his decadent reputation—though everyone had loved Harry, from porter to consultant, domestic to senior nursing staff, patient to relative, he somehow had charmed them all!

Not her, though.

Now that she thought about it, now that she sat quietly, they'd had one brief conversation away from work.

'Come on, Marnie, stop moping around…' She could hear her flatmates urging her to go out and, even though she hadn't felt like a party, to keep them from nagging, Marnie had agreed. She had stood there clutching lemonade and watching the good times unfolding as, unbeknown to her flatmates, Marnie's world fell apart. In the end she had decided to just slip away.

'Leaving so soon?'

Harry had caught her as she'd headed for the door and had offered to get her a drink. Marnie had looked into very green eyes and watched them blink as, completely impervious to his charm, without explanation, she'd simply walked off.

Marnie wondered how the charming Harry would be faring these days! He'd be in his late thirties by now—surely all those years of excess would have caught up with him. Marnie stood and turned on the shower, aiming the water on the walls and laughing to herself at the thought of a ruddy-faced Harry, who surely by now had a paunch.

Oh, and a single father to twins.

There'd been no chance then of him charming her and there'd be even less now—she could truly think of nothing worse than a single father.

Marnie was decidedly free and single and liked her men to be the same.

Selfish, some might think, not that Marnie cared a jot what others thought.

As evening descended, perhaps the light was just being kind but the place looked far nicer than it had when she had arrived. Though Marnie would never admit the same to Dave when she spoke to him about it on Monday, she actually liked the main bedroom—it had high ceilings and a huge bay window, as well as a fireplace, which would surely be gorgeous for snuggling up in bed with a good book or a man in winter.

Not that she would be here in winter, Marnie reminded herself. She would see this lease out, given she had been foolish enough to sign, but she would be finding herself a new home and Dave certainly wouldn't be her agent of choice.

Marnie made her final trip to the car and pulled out her yoga mat, which would serve as her mattress tonight, a duvet and pillow, and a box of personal effects.

Marnie set out her toiletries in the now sparkling bathroom and had a shower then headed to the main bedroom. There she put out her clothes for the morning and set up her bed for the night. Then she put her photos up on the mantelpiece.

First she put up the family favourite—Marnie and

her parents with her five younger brothers, all together on the day Ronan had graduated.

Ronan, her youngest brother, was unashamedly Marnie's favourite. She had been nearly eleven when he was born and Marnie had had a lot to do with raising him—changing his nappies, getting up to him at night, feeding him before she went to school. It was funny to think of Ronan now at twenty-one—he was a gorgeous geek who loved computers and playing the piano, though not necessarily in that order.

Marnie placed the photo above the fire and took out another. There she was, a fourteen-year-old Marnie with her best friend Siobhan on the day the Johnsons had left Ireland to emigrate to Perth, Australia, and start a new life. Though the two young girls were smiling in the photo, Marnie could see the tears in both their eyes—for Marnie and Siobhan it had been a terribly difficult time. Marnie hadn't wanted to leave her home, her school, her dancing and her friends, especially Siobhan. Still, she had made the best of it and had started to make friends—only then her father's work had dictated that the family again up sticks and move from Perth to Melbourne.

'You'll soon make new friends,' her mother had again insisted.

Yes, Marnie had made new friends but none had come close to Siobhan.

Marnie chose wisely and so when she gave her heart it was for ever and she and Siobhan were still best friends nearly twenty years later. They shared daily emails and video-called often, as well as catching up every couple of years face to face. Marnie smiled as she put out the photo and was still smiling when she pulled out the last one—but maybe it had been a long day, because she felt the sting of tears at the back of her eyes. Marnie cried rarely and she hadn't expected to feel that way today. She was tired, she reasoned, as she gazed on the familiar and much-loved photograph of an eighteen-year-old Marnie holding Declan.

Finally holding Declan.

It was such a bitter-sweet time because until he had been two weeks old Marnie had never got to hold him, though her body had ached to, her breasts leaking as much as her eyes as she'd peered into the incubator and craved the feeling of holding her son in her arms. Until the day of the photo his tiny body had been smothered in tubes and equipment but, when it had been deemed that nothing more could be done for Declan, they had all been taken away. She and Craig had been given a comfortable room away from the hustle and bustle of the neonatal unit and had had a few precious hours alone with him.

Her parents Marnie had allowed in only briefly.

'There will be time for other babies.' No, her mother hadn't been insensitive enough to say it on that day. It had been said when Marnie had first told her she was pregnant—that there would be plenty of time for other babies later down the track had been a large portion of her mother's advice.

No, there would be no other babies.

Declan was her son and he forever had her heart.

Marnie ran her finger over the image and felt not the cold of the glass but the soft warmth of her baby's skin. She looked into his dark blue eyes that were so weary from fighting and, just as she did every night, Marnie said goodnight to him.

Setting the photo down, Marnie set her alarm for six

and then settled down on her yoga mat to get ready for an uncomfortable night, sleeping on the floor.

Not that she minded.

Yes, Marnie had been through far worse.

CHAPTER TWO

'I THINK YOU'VE already met Marnie...' Lillian, the director of nursing, said as she introduced Marnie to Dr Vermont.

'I have.' The elderly doctor shook her hand and Marnie smiled back at him warmly. 'We met at Marnie's first interview. I was thrilled to hear that you had accepted the position,' he added to Marnie. 'Hopefully you can bring some order to the place.'

'I have every intention to.' Marnie smiled again. She had, on sight, liked Dr Vermont. He was old school and liked things done a certain way and had had no qualms in telling her such, which was exactly how Marnie liked to work.

'Harry!' Lillian called, and Marnie turned to the sight of Harry Worthington, fast realising that instead of his wild youth catching up with him, he had left it behind, only to improve. Rather than the scrubs she remembered him wearing, that tall, muscular physique was now dressed in a well-cut charcoal-grey suit. He seemed taller, a touch broader, but there was far from a paunch; if anything, he was slimmer than the Harry of yesteryear. He wasn't quite perfection. It was no longer designer stubble that graced his jaw—Harry needed a good shave! He also needed to put on a tie. He had an unfinished look to him that ten minutes would soon take care of. Perhaps, though, the most surprising thing to see was that the once terribly sexy, laid-back Harry was now late and clearly rushing with a little boy and girl hanging off each hand as Lillian made the introductions.

'This is Marnie Johnson, the new nurse unit manager. You didn't manage to come in for her interviews.'

'No, I was on night duty for the first and on a day off for the other,' Harry explained, 'but Dr Vermont has said many good things about you.' He let go of his daughter and shook Marnie's hand, albeit briefly, because the little girl, as soon as she was let loose, started to wander off.

'Charlotte!' Harry warned, giving a brief eye-roll to Marnie before retrieving his daughter's hand. 'How many times do I have to tell you? You're to stay with me.'

'But I'm hungry.'

'That's because you didn't eat your cornflakes,' Harry said to his daughter as he returned to the group, and Marnie watched as Lillian's lips pursed in disapproval. Marnie couldn't see that there was an issue—clearly, Harry had just arrived for work and was taking his children to day care. It was hardly his fault that there was a group to meet him.

'You and Marnie might already have met.' Lillian pushed on with the conversation when really it would be far easier to make the introductions once Harry didn't have his children with him. 'Marnie, didn't you train at Melbourne Central?'

Harry frowned. He looked at Marnie's raven hair and china-blue eyes and couldn't quite believe they might have worked alongside each other for three years and that he didn't recognise her at all.

'No,' Marnie corrected Lillian. 'I only did my first year of training at Melbourne Central. After that I transferred to the Royal.' She turned to Harry. 'I do remember you, though...' Marnie said, and suppressed a smile at the slight flare of concern in his eyes—perhaps Harry might be a little uncomfortable with people who could remember him in his wilder days.

Perhaps, Marnie thought, noticing again, after all these years, his stunning green eyes, it was time for some fun. Dr Vermont was talking to Harry's son and Lillian was briefly distracted by her pager going off and Marnie simply could not resist a tease, even though they had barely ever spoken. 'You remember me, though, don't you?'

'Actually...' Harry let go of Charlotte's hand again as he rather worriedly scratched at the back of his neck. 'Now I think back on it...'

'Surely you remember,' Marnie implored, enjoying herself.

'Charlotte!' Harry called, but Marnie could hear the relief in his voice at a brief chance of escape.

'I'm just about to take Marnie on a tour and introduce her to everyone,' Lillian interrupted the fun. 'Marnie, do you want to go and get your jacket before I show you around?'

'I'm fine.' Marnie shook her head. 'We'll just get on.'

But Lillian had other ideas. 'We actually like the managers to wear their jackets, especially for things like formal introductions—it adds a nice authoritative touch.'

'I don't need a jacket to be authoritative,' Marnie responded, and it was Harry who was suppressing a smile now as he watched her walk off.

Not many people spoke to Lillian like that.

Clearly Marnie was setting the tone.

'I think,' Dr Vermont said as Marnie clipped off with Lillian moving fast to catch up, 'that Marnie Johnson might be just what the doctor ordered—did you see Lillian's face when she said that she didn't need a jacket?'

'I did.' Harry grinned.

'So, do you remember her from Melbourne Central?'

'I don't.' Harry swallowed, paying great attention to Adam and failing to see the twinkle in Dr Vermont's eyes.

'She seems to remember you!'

'I'd better get these two over to day care,' Harry said, again glad of the excuse of the twins to escape. He walked behind Marnie and Lillian on his way to day care, trying and failing not to notice her very petite, trim figure in the navy dress. She had stopped to shake hands with Juan Morales, one of the new consultants who was just finishing up after a night shift. 'And Dr Cooper starts when?' Harry heard Marnie asking as he walked past.

'In four weeks' time, I believe,' Juan answered.

Harry didn't hang around to hear the rest of the conversation. Just wait until Lillian and Marnie found out that he had approved Juan's annual leave, commencing in one week's time! Yes, the place was almost running well with Juan finally on board, but it was all about to go to pot again some time soon.

Harry signed his name alongside Charlotte's and Adam's in the day-care register and tried to focus on today instead of worrying about the weeks ahead.

Since Jill had died, he had learnt that it was the best he could do.

'Are you picking us up?' Adam asked.

'I'll do my best to be here at six,' Harry said. 'But if

it looks as if I won't be able to get away on time, I will ring Evelyn and she'll pick you up.'

Harry could not stand Adam's nod, or that his son was trying not to cry. He knelt down to look Adam in the eye. 'We had a good weekend, didn't we?'

They'd had a brilliant weekend—the first in ages.

With Juan working, both Harry and Dr Vermont had finally had a full, undisturbed weekend without being rung for advice or called in urgently. Dr Vermont had taken his wife away to celebrate their upcoming wedding anniversary, which fell today. He himself had taken his children to the beach on the Saturday and had spent Sunday finally tackling the garden then watching movies in the evening.

Simple pleasures perhaps, but they hadn't shared a weekend so straightforward in ages.

'I just...' Adam started, but he didn't finish and Harry waited. He was worried about Adam's talking, or rather the lack of it. 'It doesn't matter,' Adam said.

Oh, but it did.

Harry looked at Adam's dark, serious eyes, so like his mum's. And, like Jill, Adam never complained about Harry's ridiculous work hours, which only served to make Harry feel worse. 'Hey,' Harry said. 'Tonight we're going to take those bruised bananas and make banana bread.' It was completely off the top of his head. 'So tomorrow you and Charlotte will have something nice waiting for breakfast that you can eat in the car if we're in a hurry.'

'Promise?' Adam checked.

'As much as I can promise,' Harry said, because the very nature of his job meant that nothing could be guaranteed. 'But if we don't get to make it tonight then the bananas will be even blacker tomorrow and the banana bread even sweeter.'

Finally, Adam smiled.

'I hate banana bread!' Charlotte, the louder of the two, had to have her say as Harry gave her a kiss goodbye.

'I know.' Harry smiled. 'But you do like eating the frosting.'

'Can I make the frosting?' Charlotte was more easily cheered, though, unlike Adam and Jill, she did protest loudly whenever Harry was late picking them up or was called into work.

'Yep,' Harry said, and then, because he had to, he qualified again. 'If I get home in time.'

'Try,' Charlotte said.

It was all he seemed to be doing these days.

He hugged them both and then, as good as gold, they headed off to join their little friends to start their very long day.

Something had to give.

Harry headed back towards the department and tried, for now, not to think about the unpalatable decision that he was coming to.

As well as being an emergency consultant, Harry was also a renowned hand surgeon. He was reluctantly considering moving into the private sphere and focusing on his second love—hands. Emergency and single fatherhood, he had fast found out, simply didn't mix.

Harry had decided that he was going to take some annual leave while he made his decision. Once Juan was back from his honeymoon and Dr Cooper had started work and the department was adequately staffed, he could take some proper time off and work out what to do.

He just needed to get through the next few weeks.

Harry headed straight for the changing rooms and took the ten minutes Marnie had noted that he needed. He quickly shaved, combed his hair and added a tie, then walked back into the department, and the first person he saw was Marnie.

'That's better!' Marnie commented, when others perhaps would not have.

'Better?'

'You've shaved, put on a tie…'

'I don't need a tie to be a consultant.' Harry made light reference to her jacket comment to Lillian but still he bristled. She should see how Juan dressed some days, stomping about in Cuban-heeled boots, and, until recently, Juan's black hair had been longer than shoulder length—imagine what she'd have had to say about that! Harry had always prided himself on his appearance and tried to look smart for work, and he really didn't need a lecture today.

Heading to her office, Marnie gave it a good wipe down with alcohol rubs and then, deciding it was too drab, she rang a local florist and asked for flowers to be delivered. Then she asked Cate Nicholls, who had been filling in after Christine had left, to bring her up to date with certain protocols and paperwork.

'Most multi-trauma goes straight to the city, though it depends on transport availability, so we can get a sudden influx,' Cate explained, but Marnie had gone through most of this at her interviews. The paperwork took a while—there were all the patient complaints and staff incident reports to go through.

'They're mainly about waiting times,' Cate commented.

'And cleanliness,' Marnie observed, flicking through

them. 'Is there a protocol for cubicle preparation for the patients?'

'Not one that's written as such,' Cate said.

There soon would be! Still, Marnie moved on to the budget lists and all the stuff that Cate had loathed but which Marnie just loved to tackle.

'I hope everything is up to date,' Cate said. 'If it's not…'

'I'll just ask you,' Marnie answered.

'I won't be around, though,' Cate reminded her. 'I'm going on annual leave next week.'

'Of course, you're getting married…are you going anywhere nice for your honeymoon?'

'We're getting married in Argentina,' Cate answered. 'Juan and I—'

'You're marrying Juan?'

'That's right.'

'The new doctor?' Marnie checked, and Cate nodded.

'How long are you going to be away for?'

'Three weeks.'

Cate was still smiling. Perhaps, as most would be, she was waiting for congratulations—she just didn't know Marnie, whose only interest at work was work. 'Are you saying that Juan's got three weeks off!' Marnie exclaimed. 'But he's only just started.'

By nine a.m. both Lillian and Cate had glimpsed what was to come.

By midday the rest of the staff were starting to.

'Are there four of her?' Kelly, one of the nurses, grumbled as she sat on a stool beside Harry.

'Sorry?' Harry looked up from the notes he was writing. 'Four of who?'

'Marnie.' Kelly sighed. 'It seems that everywhere I go, there she is.'

Harry grinned. Marnie certainly wasn't hiding in the office, as Christine had—she darted in and out and wherever you looked it seemed that she was there.

Harry *had* noticed and, as if to prove Kelly's point, Marnie soon appeared.

'Where are the nursing roster request forms kept?' Marnie asked Kelly.

'In here.' Kelly opened a drawer and pulled out a large diary, which Marnie took.

Then Marnie sat on a stool at a computer, quietly working her way through the rosters before disappearing.

'See!' Kelly said. 'She's everywhere...' She launched into another moan but her voice trailed off as Marnie returned with not just a new diary but instructions.

'From now on, all of the off-duty requests are to be written in the new diary, along with a reason for requesting that date,' Marnie said, as she pinned up a laminated note stating the same. 'If you would prefer to speak to me personally, rather than write your reasons down, that's fine.'

Satisfied the note was up straight, she turned and Harry realised that, though the nursing rosters had nothing at all to do with him, he was watching her. He quickly looked away, telling himself he hadn't just been admiring the rear view of the new nurse manager and the way her dress had lifted just a fraction as she'd pinned up the note.

Surely he'd remember if anything had ever happened between them?

Surely?

'Do you have a moment?' Marnie asked.

'Sure.'

'Not here.'

Harry had guessed this would be coming—Cate had warned him that Marnie had been less than impressed about Juan taking time off. With a slight roll of his eyes he headed to her office and took a seat, leaning back in the chair and stretching out his legs, absolutely refusing to jump through hoops for Marnie, as everyone else seemed to be.

'I was just looking through the doctors' roster and it would seem that we are very short of senior medical staff.'

'We have been,' Harry said. 'But things are steadily improving. We've got Juan now and there's another new consultant—Dr Cooper—starting soon.'

'Which would be great but I've just found out that Juan has been given three weeks' annual leave, starting well before Dr Cooper commences.'

'He's going home to Argentina—you can hardly go there for a long weekend.'

'But that will leave us with just you and Dr Vermont to cover the department.'

'I'm aware of that.' Harry was more than aware—things had only just started improving and now the nightmare was going to begin all over again, not that he was going to reveal the logistical nightmare to Marnie. 'Juan's getting married,' Harry pointed out, assuming that there the discussion would end.

He just didn't know Marnie.

'Could he not have delayed his wedding till Dr Cooper had started?'

'It was a whirlwind romance,' Harry answered with a wry smile.

'Please!' She rolled her eyes. 'There's no such thing and, even if there was, surely true love could at least wait a month.'

'Apparently not!' Harry said. 'Look, Juan is an amazing doctor and believe me when I say such a highly skilled doctor is usually pretty hard to entice to come and work at Bayside Hospital. Once immigration and everything is sorted, Juan's going to be a huge asset to the place but he only agreed to take the role if I accommodated his annual leave request.'

'You *acquire* annual leave,' Marnie said. 'Juan hasn't acquired any, from what I can see.'

Harry tried a different tack. 'The guy broke his neck a while back, he was barely able to walk when he got to Australia. As well as getting married, he really wants to return home and let his family see how well he's doing.'

Oh, but Marnie was having none of it. 'So Juan breaking his neck means you have to bend over backwards and break yours to accommodate his love life?'

Harry was sure then that he hadn't slept with her!

He'd certainly remember—Harry had never met anyone like her in his life! 'You're not a romantic, I take it?' Harry's voice was dry.

'There's not a single romantic bone in my body,' Marnie said. 'But so long as you can assure me that the department will be adequately covered with senior medical staff then it's not my issue.'

'It will be covered.'

'Good.'

Harry stood up and turned to go, but how well they might have known each other was driving him crazy, so he decided to simply bite the bullet and ask, 'What year were you at Melbourne Central?'

'You really don't remember?' Marnie said. 'I was blonde then, if that helps.'

'Blonde?' Harry looked at her very thick black hair. 'That would have taken some peroxide.'

'It did,' Marnie said. 'You still don't remember me, do you?'

She loved his discomfort—loved the small swallow in his neck—and she watched as he drew in a breath while attempting to come up with a suitable answer. Then those green eyes met hers and a smile spread on Harry's lips, lips that had been just a little insolent and teasing in their day, Marnie recalled, and they were becoming that now.

'How could I ever forget you, Marnie?'

The little game Marnie had been playing had suddenly gone too far because it was Marnie, most unusually, who struggled to calm a blush, and she rapidly decided to put an end to it, while still keeping the upper hand. 'It's okay, Harry, I've been teasing you. You don't have to worry—I'm very possibly the only student nurse at Melbourne Central that you didn't sleep with.'

'Glad to hear it,' Harry said, still smiling back at her, except the smile sort of wavered, because maybe that wasn't the right answer to give.

What was the right answer to a statement like that? Harry wondered as he walked off.

He couldn't make Marnie out. She was a strange mix. Forthright yet distant, funny yet stern but, even if he was smiling at the little game she'd played on him, Harry knew as he headed back to the patients that the holiday was over. Not that you could ever call this place a holiday, but there would be no asking Marnie if she could keep an eye out for the twins in the staffroom, even if it was right near her office. There would be no appealing to her feminine side and asking her to grab them from day care, or would she mind if one of the nurses in the obs ward kept an eye on them for an hour.

Harry just knew it.

CHAPTER THREE

YES, MARNIE WAS everywhere.

As Harry sat having his lunch he found out, if he hadn't known already, just how forthright she was—the pint-sized Marnie didn't even try to mince her words when she answered a personal call.

Marnie didn't excuse herself from the staffroom to take the call—instead, she tucked the phone between her neck and chin and squirted salad dressing over her home-made salad. As she thanked Dave for returning her call, she stirred in the dressing.

Oh, her accent was as soft as butter as she spoke but you could almost feel it choking the rather unfortunate Dave's arteries.

'Absolutely, I signed the contract but let me ask you this, Dave—was one month's rent really worth it? I certainly shan't be staying on when my lease is up.' Harry listened as she made it very clear that she wouldn't be using him in the future and hopefully, if the hospital grapevine served her well, neither would anybody else from Bayside. 'So, to be clear,' Marnie concluded, 'you have my notice and I have photos of before and after so I'll be expecting to receive my deposit in full—the place was nothing but a filthy swamp before I set to work.'

'Ripped off?' Kelly asked, and Marnie nodded.

'It's my own fault for signing a lease on a place that I hadn't seen. He only showed me the first half of Beach Road...' She didn't elaborate and she didn't sit around for much longer—after finishing her salad, Marnie stood and left the staffroom.

'I can't make up my mind whether or not I like her,' Kelly grumbled.

'Well, I've made up my mind and I don't.' Abby, another of the nurses, sighed. 'I was given a ten-minute lesson on the correct way to wash my hands, as if I didn't already know. I think that she's got OCD!'

'She's got ADHD,' Kelly grumbled. 'She just never stops.'

'Ladies!' Dr Vermont said, and didn't even look up from his newspaper as he delivered a warning for the nurses to stop gossiping.

Though, a few hours later, he indulged in a little gossip of his own as he put on his jacket to head for home. 'What do you think of Marnie?' Dr Vermont asked Harry.

'I don't know what to think,' Harry admitted. 'She's not exactly here to make friends, is she? Marnie doesn't seem to care who she offends.'

'I like that about her,' Dr Vermont said. 'The trouble with Christine was that she was either your best friend or your worst enemy.' He thought about it for a long moment. 'I know that it's very early days but so far I'm impressed.'

Dr Vermont was more than a colleague to Harry. He was a friend and mentor and Harry admired him greatly. If Dr Vermont liked Marnie, that was high praise indeed and almost as good as a reference.

'Well, so far so good,' Harry conceded. 'But enough about this place—hadn't you better get going?'

'Sorry that I have to dash off.' Dr Vermont didn't elaborate. They both knew that it was his wedding anniversary today and Dr Vermont was kind enough to realise that milestones such as the one he and Marjorie had just reached might cause a twinge of pain for Harry.

'You go and enjoy yourself,' Harry smiled. 'Forty years is quite an achievement.'

'I know that it is,' Dr Vermont agreed. 'We've got all the family coming over tonight…' He paused as Harry took a beautifully wrapped bottle from his desk and handed it to him.

'Well, you'd better hide this from them, then.'

Dr Vermont thanked Harry and after he had gone to celebrate with his wife and family Harry sat for a long moment.

Jill had been dead now for more than a year and a half. Birthdays and two Christmases had passed. Two wedding anniversaries had been and gone as well—and still it hurt. Some days more, some days less, but the pain was always there. Not just for Jill and all that she was missing out on, but for himself and more pointedly for the twins. Harry twisted the ring on his finger—he still couldn't bring himself to take it off. It wasn't just the hurt, there was also guilt—perpetual, constant guilt about whether or not he was doing a good job with the children. Certainly they weren't being brought up as Jill would have wanted. She had wanted to stay home at least until the twins had started school.

Yes, he was doing his best—he was just all too aware that it wasn't quite enough.

Harry headed back out to the department, which was, for once, quiet. The late staff were all trying to pretend to be busy as Marnie sat at the nurses' station and went through the policy manual, and of course she was making notes and had several questions for Harry.

'Sheldon just brought back a puncture wound of the hand for review in the hand clinic tomorrow.' Marnie had been surprised; it was a very small injury that could easily have been followed up by a GP. 'When I questioned him he said it was policy. Now I've checked and it says here that all hand injuries, regardless of how small, are to be brought back the next day for review in the hand clinic.'

'That's right.'

'All?'

'All.' Harry nodded. 'A lot of things get picked up in the hand clinic and for the most part the patients are in and out in less than a minute. It's worth it, though, because something that seemed minor at the time is often picked up. I've found it works better to just bring everyone with a hand injury, no matter how small, back the next day for review.'

'Fair enough.' Marnie turned the page and then glanced up at the clock. 'What time do you finish?'

'Now,' Harry said. 'Day care closes at six.'

'Dr Morales comes on at nine?' Marnie checked.

'That's right. Though you can call me for anything you're concerned about—all of the staff know that.'

'They do,' Marnie said. 'I'll see you tomorrow, then.'

'You shall.' Harry smiled. 'It's nice to meet you, Marnie, and I'm very glad that we never...' He halted. He wished he could take that back and wondered what had possessed him to even go there in the first place.

'New girl's tease.' Marnie smiled. 'I couldn't help myself.'

'I thought it was supposed to be the other way around, that we were supposed to be teasing you.'

'I make my own fun,' Marnie said.

She really was the oddest mix and, if there was any doubt as to that, she proved it when she continued talking. 'I should be offended really that you're so relieved nothing ever happened.' Marnie winked. ''Night, Harry.'

He turned to go but as he did so the alert phone rang and Miriam, one of the late staff, took the call. 'There's a multi-trauma coming in, they've just diverted and are bringing him here,' Miriam said. 'ETA ten minutes. Harry, would you like me to run over and grab the twins for you?'

'That would be great,' Harry said, taking off his jacket but pausing midway as Marnie's soft voice carried the length of the nurses' station and promptly halted everyone.

'Instead of running over to day care, Miriam, shouldn't you be setting up for the multi-trauma?'

Miriam hesitated and when Harry gave her a nod, instead of racing to get the twins, Miriam headed into Resus.

'You'd better get going,' Marnie said to Harry. 'You don't want to get caught up in this.'

No, he didn't want to get caught up but if it was serious he would call for the trauma team to come down and if it wasn't serious Sheldon could deal with it, except Marnie was already speaking into the phone.

'Could you fast-page the trauma team to come to Emergency?' she said, but as she replaced the receiver Harry was waiting for her.

'They might not be needed.'

'Hopefully not,' Marnie said, 'but if they are then surely it's better for the patient to have them waiting here.'

Harry heard the overhead intercom crackle into life to summon the team.

''Night, Harry,' Marnie said again.

For Harry it was the strangest feeling to be leaving the department knowing full well there was an emergency on its way in.

He was always running towards an emergency; instead, this evening, he was walking away.

It just didn't feel right.

And however assured Marnie was, he couldn't help but wonder how she'd deal with a less-than-impressed trauma team if she'd called them at five to six for something minor, just when they were due to go home…

Harry paused as he reached day care, dropped one ball from the many he was juggling as he heard the sound of his colleagues' footsteps racing down the corridor to greet whatever was being brought in.

Harry let out a breath and walked into day care. No, he wasn't the first parent to get there but at least he wasn't the last.

'Daddy! We thought you'd have to help with the emergency!' Charlotte squealed, and flung herself at him. Her brown curls were bobbing and her green eyes, the same as her dad's, were smiling with excitement as she realised it was home time. *And* she remembered the promises made.

'Can I make the frosting?'

'You can.'

Even though the trauma team was arriving, the blasted intercom was summoning the team for the second time as Harry signed the twins out.

As he walked down the corridor, carrying Charlotte and holding Adam's hand, he felt Adam still as the stretcher was raced in. He looked down and saw Adam blinking. 'He'll be okay,' Harry assured him.

But the injured man on the stretcher didn't upset Adam, he'd seen way more than most children had already. No, he was bracing himself for his father to return them to day care, Harry realised, or to pop them around to the staffroom; instead, they headed to the car.

'Who's looking after him?' Adam checked, because normally his father was needed.

'He's going to be fine,' Harry said, wishing for the hundredth time his children didn't know or see so much, but the hospital day-care centre was his only choice if he was going to work here. 'There is a team of specialists waiting for him.'

Harry strapped the twins into their car seats and drove the short distance home as Charlotte filled him in on her day, talking non-stop till they were turning into their street.

'How about your day, Adam?' Harry asked, trying to encourage Adam to speak.

'We did paintings.' Adam looked at his father as if Harry must have briefly lost his mind. 'Charlotte just told you.'

'I know.' Harry smiled. They were just so different. Charlotte liked every gap in the conversation filled with her voice, whereas Adam was only too happy to sit back and listen.

Evelyn came out to help him with the twins as they pulled into the driveway, but as she ushered them in, knowing he wouldn't be able to relax till he knew things were okay at work, Harry told Evelyn he'd join them soon. He stood in the hallway, took out his phone and called Emergency. It was Marnie who answered.

'How's the multi-trauma?' Harry asked.

'All good,' Marnie replied. 'Well, not so good if you're the patient, but it's all under control. He's just heading round for an MRI.'

'I can come back if you need me,' Harry said. 'My babysitter's here.'

'There's really no point,' Marnie said. 'As I said, it's all under control. The team have been fantastic.'

'Shouldn't you be at home?' Harry asked, glancing at his watch. She'd been there since long before nine after all.

'Shouldn't you be?' Marnie asked, and Harry gave a thin smile as he heard the chatter coming from the kitchen.

Marnie had made a very good point.

Happy that the patient was being well looked after, Harry headed into the kitchen and to the delicious scent of dinner. 'Smells good,' Harry said.

'I'm trying something different.' Evelyn smiled at the twins. 'Tonight we're eating Russian!'

'Ooh!' Charlotte was delighted, Adam not so sure, and Harry was simply grinning because Evelyn was so Australian she thought beef stroganoff was exotic.

Having Evelyn look after the children had, absolutely, been the best idea Harry had had.

Actually, it had been Juan's idea that he get an older carer for the children.

Yep, *mea culpa*, Harry had slept with the last nanny and the one before that.

It was exhausting being a widower at times!

Seriously.

Harry didn't want a wife—he'd had Jill. Sex, though, that was another matter entirely. Why did women always have to complicate things by falling in love?

At least Evelyn didn't read a single thing into it when

Harry suggested that instead of dashing off she join them for dinner.

'Are you sure?' Evelyn checked, but she was already pulling out a chair. 'How was work?'

'Good,' Harry said, because, given he was home on time, it must have been a good day. 'We've got a new nurse manager just started,' Harry said. 'She seems very efficient.'

'She's rude,' Charlotte said.

'Rude?' Harry looked at his daughter, who was spooning sour cream onto her dinner, and tried to recall them meeting her. 'How can you say Marnie's rude? You barely even met her.'

'She didn't say hello to us,' Charlotte said.

'It was her first day,' Harry commented. 'I'm sure she had other things to think of.' Though, as Harry wrestled the sour cream from Charlotte, he did dwell on it for just a second. Charlotte was right, well, not the rude part but usually people did comment on the twins, especially when they realised that they were twins. Charlotte, Harry decided, was just far too used to having people drop to their knees and tell her how cute she was.

Dinner was nice and Harry refused Evelyn's offer to stay and do the dishes. 'I can stack a dishwasher!' Harry said, as he saw her to the door.

'If you need me tonight,' Evelyn offered, 'you just have to call.'

'I shan't tonight,' Harry said. 'Juan's on. Things might get a bit busy, though, once he's off on his honeymoon.'

'No problem.'

Evelyn really was fantastic, Harry thought as he saw her out. Evelyn was their next-door-but-one neighbour. She had lost her husband many years ago and desperately missed her daughter, who had moved with her husband and baby to China. Evelyn had actually cried when Harry had taken up Juan's suggestion to get someone older and Harry had asked if she could be there for the twins.

For cash!

Perfect.

Evelyn was saving up to go and visit her family in China and she got to spoil Charlotte and Adam in the interim.

The twins went to day care but on the odd day they were sick, Evelyn was there, and if Harry was on call, Evelyn slept in the nanny's room. She didn't even mind the odd time when Harry had to call her during the night.

It wasn't a complete solution but for now it was working.

Wow!

It was just after seven. Dinner was done and the dishwasher was on.

'Can we make the banana bread?' Adam asked.

'Yep.'

Oh, the bliss of the absence of parental guilt, Harry thought as Adam mashed bananas. In no time there was the lovely scent of banana bread filling the house as he got the twins bathed and ready for bed.

'The frosting!' Charlotte said. 'You promised that I could make the frosting.'

'I know, but the bread had to cool.' Harry looked up the recipe on the Internet and squeezed some orange juice, which Charlotte mashed into cream cheese. By nine p.m. the twins were in bed, there was a slice of banana bread wrapped for Adam's breakfast and a small bowl of frosting for Charlotte. And there was just a glimpse of order to the home for the first time in a very long time.

Harry lay back on the couch and yawned.

They'd made it through another day.

He thought of Marnie stopping Miriam from going to fetch the children, and the strangest thing was he was actually grateful for it. Harry didn't want people rushing to pick up his children and he loathed all the favours that he constantly had to ask.

It was Marnie who had done him a true favour today.

She'd given him an evening at home with the twins.

CHAPTER FOUR

'EXCUSE ME!'

Harry's tongue rolled in his cheek as he heard Marnie's beguilingly soft voice. She walked over to Sheldon, the resident, who was washing his hands at the surgical sink.

Poor Sheldon, he had no idea what was coming.

Harry did. Marnie had delivered Harry exactly the same lecture she was now giving Sheldon.

'You see these long taps, Sheldon?'

'Yes.'

'Well, it might surprise you to hear that they're not designed for helping doctors who happen to have big hands.'

Harry couldn't resist looking up. He could see Sheldon blushing and Marnie smiling as she delivered a very firm lecture but in the sweetest voice. 'And, neither were they designed for busy doctors so that they could just push them back quickly. The designers were far more thoughtful than that—do you know why the taps are so long, Sheldon?'

'Okay, Marnie, I get it,' Sheldon said through gritted teeth.

'But I don't think that you do. You see, they're designed that way so that you can turn them on and off with your elbows. I'll show you...'

'I already know,' Sheldon said as Marnie demonstrated how to turn the taps on and off with her own elbows.

'You know that?' Marnie checked. 'I'm so sorry, Sheldon, I didn't think you did because when I saw you just washing your hands...'

Harry shook his head and got back to his notes as Marnie continued to give Sheldon a lesson on handwashing. She was obsessed with cleanliness and handwashing was at the top of her list, along with cleaning the curtains and light switches.

'What,' Marnie had demanded, 'is the point of cleaning your hands and then opening a filthy curtain with them?'

Oh, and she had a thing about sunlight.

'It's cheaper than bleach,' Marnie had said when she had called Maintenance down to prise open windows that had never, in all the time Harry had been there, been opened. 'Sunlight kills everything.'

In the two weeks that Marnie had been at Bayside she had turned the *Titanic*.

The place was glistening, the cupboards were well stocked, and breaks were being taken, though heaven help you if you left the kitchen without washing and putting away your coffee cup.

Love her or loathe her, there was no doubt that the place was well run under Marnie's command and, as a consultant in the busy emergency department, Harry should be feeling extremely pleased at that fact.

He was pleased.

It was just...

Marnie did not give an inch. No, Harry didn't want

favours, but a bit of flexibility wouldn't go amiss either. With Juan now in Argentina and Dr Cooper's starting date still a few weeks away, for Dr Vermont and Harry the wheels were again starting to come off. They were relying heavily on locums—some were excellent, others not. But locums were exactly that, they didn't have the investment in the place that the regular staff had. Sheldon, for one, was becoming increasingly exasperated about who the latest boss was and at what point he should call the regular senior staff in.

'Marnie!' Harry heard the surprise in Sheldon's voice and looked up as Sheldon spoke on. 'Did anyone ever tell you that you could be a hand model?'

'I get told it all the time!' Marnie said.

'I'm serious.' Sheldon was turning her hands over and examining them. 'They're amazing.'

'I know they are,' Marnie said. 'Really, I should just take the plunge and get them insured and go off and make my fortune.'

'Harry,' Sheldon called, 'have you seen Marnie's hands?'

'Er, no,' Harry lied. He'd noticed them when Marnie had given him the little hand-washing lecture the other day and Sheldon was right—they were incredible. Her skin was unblemished and pale, with long, slender fingers that tapered into very neat, oval nails. They really were beautiful.

'Show Harry,' Sheldon said.

Marnie duly walked over and held out her hands. Emergency was a mad place at times, so this sort of thing wasn't in the least peculiar. Even Kelly came over to admire Marnie's hands.

'They're lovely,' Harry said.

'Harry's got a bit of a *thing* about hands,' Kelly

teased, but even she was surprised when Marnie took it a stage further.

'Do they turn you on, Harry?' Marnie said. Harry couldn't help but smile back and Kelly gave a slightly shocked laugh. Marnie was a minx—sexy yet cold, flirtatious at times but only when it suited her mood. And... Harry liked her.

Yes, it was another reason Harry wasn't feeling best pleased. Liking Marnie was too inconvenient for words.

'I have an *interest* in hands,' Harry said, and Marnie smirked at his response, 'not a fetish.'

'You *really* should be a hand model,' Kelly said, peering at them and then at her own.

'And who would keep you lot in place?' Marnie asked. 'Though I do know what you mean. Sometimes I look down at them and find myself smiling.'

No one was smiling a little while later when the nursing off-duty was revealed. It was the first one Marnie had done and a group of nurses had fallen on the diary the moment that it had appeared.

Abby, who loathed night duty, found that she was about to do her first stint after two years of having managed to avoid it.

Harry, who should be moving on to the next patient, couldn't help but stretch out his patient notes just so that he could listen as Abby voiced her concerns to Marnie.

Of course, they fell on deaf ears.

'I hate nights too.' Marnie smiled. 'Which is one of the reasons that I went into management, though I'm doing a stint myself soon, just to see how the place runs at night. We can be miserable together.'

Harry didn't look up as Abby slunk off, only for Kelly to take her place. 'Er, Marnie...' Kelly started. 'I wrote in the request notes that I don't do early shifts at the weekends, yet you've put me down for an early shift on Saturday next week and again a fortnight later.'

'I saw that you had requested that, Kelly, but you didn't write down a reason. I really am trying my best to accommodate everyone. Why can't you do an early shift on a Saturday?'

'Well, the thing is…' Kelly attempted, and Harry listened to the discomfort in her voice as she tried to give a suitable reason. 'I like to go out on a Friday night.'

'Of course you do!' Marnie answered calmly. 'We all love to go out and get blethered on a Friday night—heaven knows, we need it after a week in this place—which is why we share around the pleasure of a lie-in on a Saturday. Everyone takes their turn.'

And with that she walked off.

'I want to loathe her,' Kelly said. 'I have every reason to loathe her and yet…'

Harry glanced up. There was Marnie, catching the poor maintenance man before he escaped as she had plenty more jobs for him.

'She's efficient,' Harry said.

'She's cold,' Kelly corrected. 'She's been here for a couple of weeks and, do you know, nobody knows one single thing about her.'

Kelly was right and it was unusual. Emergency was a place that thrived on gossip, yet Marnie just didn't partake. Yes, long before he'd noticed her beautiful hands he had noticed that there was no wedding or engagement ring. Not that that meant anything—after all, he still wore his. He'd also noticed a large bunch of flowers has been delivered on the day that she had arrived. But, as she had taken delivery and inhaled the fragrances of the bouquet, Marnie had offered no explanation as to the sender. She never spoke about last night or what her plans were for the weekend. All she really spoke about was work and yet, no matter how he tried to tell himself it didn't matter, Harry kept finding himself wanting to know a little bit more.

She was intriguing.

It was as if she looked at the world through a different end of the telescope from everyone else—a case in point was Juan. All the staff raved about Juan and how lucky Cate was, how wonderful the wedding would be and what a great catch he was.

Marnie screwed up her nose.

'He's a fine doctor, but he'd drive me bonkers to live with,' Marnie said. Everyone was trying really hard not to like her but sometimes she just lit up the department with her commentary. Just like the windows she insisted on opening, she made the drab suddenly brighter.

'But he's gorgeous,' Abby said.

'He's a bit too New Age for me and I'd get tired of him being, oh, so understanding.' Marnie seemed to think about it for a moment and then shook her head. 'Imagine trying to have a row with that…'

'So you like a good row?' Harry asked.

'Of course,' Marnie said. 'Can you imagine trying to row with Juan? "No, I don't want my shoulders massaged…"'

Yet as funny and as intriguing as she could be, Marnie was also, as Harry had guessed she would be, completely immutable in certain areas.

'Marnie…' Harry approached her after taking a call. 'Day care just rang and Adam's not feeling too well. There's still a bit of a backlog and I thought I might just pop him in the staffroom—'

'Harry,' Marnie interrupted, 'the staffroom really isn't the place for a child that is not feeling well.'

'I know that but it will only be for an hour. I'm just asking if the nurse in the obs ward could pop her head in now and then.'

'Sorry.' Marnie didn't look remotely sorry as she shook her head. 'She's got post-op patients to keep an eye on. If Adam is unwell, he needs to be at home.'

'You know…' Harry gritted his teeth and stopped the words from coming out as they reached the tip of his tongue.

'Feel free to say it,' Marnie invited.

Instead, he chose a different tack. 'Fine, if no one can keep an eye out then I'll ring my seventy-year-old babysitter and ask her to drive over…'

'Grand.'

Except, when he rang Evelyn, Harry received the worrying news that she had just been to the doctor. The rash that she hadn't told Harry about just happened to be shingles and she wouldn't be able to help out with the children for a few days at least.

'Don't worry about the kids, you just get well, Evelyn,' Harry said. He didn't want to worry Evelyn with the places his mind had suddenly gone to—namely the twins contracting chickenpox. They had been immunised, surely? But, then, Jill had seen to all that. As both a doctor and a parent Harry's mind was racing through several scenarios even as he put down the phone. 'She can't come,' a rather distracted Harry told Marnie.

'Then you'd better get Adam home.'

'You know, you really are inflexible at times,' Harry snapped.

'Oh, but I'm very flexible, Harry,' Marnie responded. 'In fact, if twenty critically ill patients came pouring through that door at this very moment you'd see just how flexible I can be. I know exactly where my staff are and what they are doing, and I can call them at any given time because they are *not* keeping an eye out for a sick child.'

She made a very good point; unfortunately, Harry was in no mood to see it. He was trying to do the best by the department and do his best by his children too. He was worried that an unwell Adam might be in the early stages of chickenpox, which meant, if he was, no doubt any day Charlotte would be too. Marnie just didn't seem to understand.

'You just don't get it,' Harry said, picking up his jacket. 'You're not a mum.'

CHAPTER FIVE

IT HURT.

And it still hurt as Marnie drove home but she did her best to push it aside when there was a knock at the door a little while later and it was her youngest brother, Ronan.

He'd just started work and was frantically saving up to move out from home, but every now and then he came and stayed for a couple of days with Marnie.

'How's the new job?' Ronan asked.

'Frustrating,' Marnie said. 'It would be a great department if there were enough staff and people didn't keep using the place as a drop-in crèche…' She stopped herself from elaborating. 'Don't mind me,' Marnie said, but Harry's words were still smarting and, in no mood to make dinner, she suggested that they eat out. 'My treat,' Marnie said. 'On the condition that you have dinner waiting for me tomorrow when I get home.'

It was nice to get out. Marnie drove along the beach road and into the small town and they soon found a gorgeous pub and sat outside, overlooking the bay, in the late sunlight.

Ronan, who was permanently hungry, dived into a huge steak while Marnie had prawns and a mango salad and enjoyed just sitting back and relaxing in front of the view, as she had promised herself she would of an evening. She wouldn't trade places with anyone. Watching a family on the next table, the mother spooning puréed pumpkin into a hungry baby's mouth as the father tried to amuse an overtired toddler, Marnie was very glad to be able to simply linger over her meal with her brother. She listened as Ronan told her about his work, and then got to, perhaps, the real reason he had asked to visit.

'You know what Mum's like,' Ronan said. 'I'm just warning you that she was upset you didn't come and visit at the weekend, or the last.'

'She surely knows how busy I am with work,' Marnie said. 'And moving! She could've come and helped with the move, like you did—she knows she doesn't need a written invitation to come and see me.'

'I think that she's just upset that you've moved so far.'

'It's not as if I've gone back home to Ireland.' Marnie sighed. 'I'm an hour's drive away.'

'She thinks you're punishing her for us emigrating…' Ronan attempted to make light of it but it was a bit of a dark subject and Marnie had to push out a smile.

'I'll try and get over one evening, but…' Marnie shook her head; maybe she was avoiding her parents a bit at the moment but she just didn't want to discuss it with Ronan. Or rather she simply couldn't discuss it with anyone in her family. *That* time of the year was coming up. The time of year that no one in her family ever spoke about because no one in her family knew what to say.

Declan would soon have been thirteen.

She looked over to the little family at the next table— the toddler was eating ice cream now, the baby falling asleep on its mother's lap, and sometimes, just sometimes, she *would* like to trade places.

Marnie took a long sip of her iced water and couldn't come up with a suitable line as to why she had been avoiding her mother, so she settled for the usual instead. 'I'm just busy, Ronan.'

So too was Harry.

After an evening spent trying to find vaccination certificates, as well as asking his parents if they could have the twins for a couple of days, Harry was in no mood for a very groomed Marnie the next day. She was busily writing on the white board while telling Kelly, who was frantically fishing to find out more about the elusive new manager, that the prawns she had had last night at Peninsular Pub were the best she had tasted.

He doubted Marnie would have been eating alone.

Yes, his response was terse when Marnie had the gall to ask him how Adam was.

'He's at my parents',' Harry said. 'Along with Charlotte.'

'Is she sick as well?'

'Neither is sick. Well, Adam's got a bit of a temperature,' Harry said. 'But my babysitter has shingles and I can hardly send them to day care knowing that any minute now they could break out in spots.'

'Weren't they immunised?' She was so annoyingly practical; she might just as well have been asking if the puppies' shots were up to date.

'You'd have to ask my late wife,' Harry snapped. 'I can't find the records.'

Ooh, they bristled and they snapped their way through the day, though the animosity was put on hold when a worried-looking Kelly came over and had a word with Harry, just as Marnie was finishing checking and ordering the scheduled drugs.

'I've got a seventeen-year-old girl in who's pregnant and bleeding. Sheldon estimates her to be around twenty-four weeks. The thing is, her parents are with her and Emily keeps insisting that she doesn't want them to know that she's pregnant. They keep asking for updates and are getting really angry that I won't let them in to be with her and that the doctor hasn't been in to speak with them. I'm just not sure how to deal with patient confidentially and Sheldon's concerned...'

'I'll come now,' Harry said, but as he made to go so too did Marnie.

'I'll come with you,' Marnie said, then spoke with Kelly. 'I'm happy to deal with her and the family.'

'Please.' Kelly let out a sigh of a relief. 'I don't blame Emily a bit for not wanting to tell her parents. They're not exactly the most approachable pair.'

Emily was very young, very scared but very determined that this baby was wanted. Sheldon had already started an IV and an ultrasound machine was being wheeled in as Harry and Marnie took over. 'Reece was going to come over at the weekend and tell my parents with me,' Emily tearfully explained as Harry gently examined her abdomen. 'Do we have to tell them now?'

'Well, we don't have to tell them,' Marnie answered, 'though I think they might start to guess what the issue is when they see you strapped to a foetal monitor or they see the sign for Maternity when I take you up.' Harry saw the small smile on Emily's lips as Marnie softened things with wry humour. 'Do you not think they have an idea?'

'I'm not sure,' Emily admitted. 'Dad did say that I was putting on weight and I was about to say something but then Mum said it was because I was spending all my time sitting down, studying.' Emily started to cry. 'They're going to be so angry.'

'They're going to be concerned,' Harry said, squirting some jelly on Emily's abdomen.

Marnie bit down on her lip because, as good a doctor as Harry was, until you'd been there you simply didn't understand.

Harry hadn't been there.

Marnie had.

She took Emily's hands. 'We can tell your parents for you.'

'You don't understand…'

'I do,' Marnie said. 'Sometimes news like this is better coming from someone who's not so involved. Once they know about the baby and have calmed down, they can come in and speak with you.'

'They'll never calm down.'

'Let's just see,' Marnie said. 'For now you just worry about staying calm. The last thing we want is you stressing yourself and raising your blood pressure and things.'

'Why am I bleeding?'

'It looks as if your placenta is lying rather low,' Harry said, running the ultrasound probe over Emily's stomach, and Marnie watched Emily's face as she stared unblinking at the screen and saw her baby for the first time. 'The heartbeat is a good rate and strong,' Harry said, pointing to the screen.

'Can you tell if it's a boy or girl?'

'The one time I tried I got it wrong.' Harry smiled. 'I'm going to get the obstetricians down and they'll examine you but for now I'll let your family know what's going on, if that's okay with you?' Emily gave a wary nod and then Harry asked about Reece and got a bit of history before they left to tell her parents. Marnie gave Emily's hand a little squeeze before she left.

George and Lucia really were a rather formidable pair—the air was thick with tension as Marnie and Harry came in and sat down.

'It's ridiculous the length of time that we've been kept waiting,' George said by way of introduction.

'Well, we've been with your daughter,' Harry calmly responded. 'I just wanted to have a chat before you went in.'

'We'd like to see her,' Lucia said, instead of asking what was wrong with her daughter.

'I'd like to speak with you before you do.'

'I really just want to see her,' Lucia insisted. 'If you could just let us know what cubicle she's in.'

They knew, Marnie realised, they simply didn't want to hear it, and thankfully Harry wasted no time getting to the point.

'Emily is pregnant,' Harry said to the two rigid faces. 'We estimate that she's about twenty-four weeks, though when she sees the obstetrician she'll have a more detailed ultrasound to confirm dates.' They all sat in silence for a moment, Harry and Marnie waiting for questions as the parents awaited the doctor's solution. 'This must come as a bit of a shock,' Harry offered.

'She's in her final year at school,' George said, as if that might change things, then he turned to his wife. 'I told you that she shouldn't be seeing him. I knew this would happen.' His fists balled as he gritted his teeth. 'She's got school to think of,' George said, and then turned back to Harry. 'She can't have it.'

'Emily wants to have the baby,' Harry said, 'and, as I've said, she's about twenty-four weeks' gestation and bleeding quite heavily. She's terribly worried for her baby and frankly so am I…'

'Baby!' George simply would not accept it and Marnie was pleased this conversation was taking place well away from Emily. 'How is she supposed to take care of a baby? She's still at school herself and doing very well. She's completely messed up her life.' He started to stand and his wife went to grab his arm.

'George, please.'

'Please what?' George demanded as he started pacing. 'How the hell is she supposed to support it?'

'Sit down,' Harry said. 'The last thing Emily needs now is to be upset.'

'Well, she should have thought of that. Maybe she should think of that…' George started heading for the door but then, realising he didn't know what cubicle Emily was in, he turned to Marnie. 'You'll take me to my daughter now.'

'Emily's not allowed visitors at the moment,' Marnie responded. 'At the moment she needs calm.'

'Don't you tell me what my daughter needs.'

'I really think,' Marnie continued, 'that it might help if you go for a walk before you visit Emily, or go to the canteen, or even just sit here and get used to the idea for a little while.'

'What would you know?' George shouted, and Harry was about to step in, perhaps even get Security, because there was no way he wanted Emily being subjected to her father's anger. But Marnie didn't need his help.

'I know plenty,' Marnie said. 'I can remember every word my parents said when I was eighteen and I told them I was pregnant.' She looked at Lucia. 'My son died when he was two weeks old and, given what had been said, I wouldn't let my mother comfort me. I still can't. I can guarantee that your next conversation with your daughter will be replayed in her mind for the rest of her life.' It was Marnie who stood then. 'She's in cubicle seven but, again, I suggest that before you go in there you take some time and really *think* about the kind of parents you want to be during this difficult time for your daughter.'

Yes, she loathed bringing her private life to work but she'd loathe even more Emily's parents speaking in haste.

Marnie walked into the cubicle, glad that it appeared George wasn't following. Emily was being seen by the obstetrician but she looked over anxiously as Marnie stepped in.

'How are they?' she asked, and Marnie hoped it would soon be the other way around—with her parents asking how Emily and the baby were.

'They're just taking it all in,' she said. 'You just focus on yourself for now.'

Her parents must have been doing some thinking because it was a good half-hour later, when Emily was about to be wheeled up to Maternity, that they came in.

'You could have told me,' were her mother's first words.

'I tried,' Emily said, and now Marnie said nothing as she escorted them up to Maternity and saw Emily settled in. Steroids had been started to mature the baby's lungs in case it needed to be delivered, but for now the bleeding had slowed down and things seemed a whole lot calmer.

'Thanks, Marnie,' Emily said, once Marnie had handed over to the midwife taking over Emily's care and had popped in to say goodbye.

'I'll pop back and see you when I...' Her voice trailed

off as a very pale and clearly terrified young man came into the ward.

'I told you not to come yet,' Emily said tearfully.

'I couldn't just stay at work.'

Marnie watched as, instead of anger, George somehow found it in himself to go over and shake Reece's hand, and as Marnie headed back down to the department she knew that of all the things that had moved her about today, Reece had moved her very much. A young man who, instead of letting Emily deal with it alone, had been brave enough to leave work and come and face the music.

She could still remember the feel of Craig trembling beside her as they'd told her parents. She hadn't wanted him there but had been so proud that he had insisted on it.

Was it any wonder they had broken up even before Declan had been born?

Yet he had still been there for the birth of his son.

She could see Harry chatting to a colleague and Marnie decided she would go to lunch.

She was a touch embarrassed that she'd told her tale in front of him, but then, he wasn't the first colleague that had heard the same. Part of her job, and the reason she loved it, was that you saw people at their most raw and could actually make a difference. It had just felt a little awkward and clearly Harry thought it an issue because a few moments after she'd sat down he knocked at her office door.

'How's she doing?'

'Better,' Marnie said. 'The bleeding has stopped and the parents are a lot calmer. Her young man just arrived and George actually shook his hand.'

That wasn't what Harry was there for.

'I'm sorry for what I said yesterday,' Harry said, and he sat down when Marnie really would have preferred a more fleeting visit.

'It's really not a problem—believe me I've heard that, or similar, many times before.'

'I didn't know,' Harry said, then shook his head. 'Not that that's an excuse. I'll be more careful when I say things like that in the future.'

'Good.' She gave a small smile; he really did look uncomfortable and that had never been her intention. 'Harry, I don't broadcast what happened to me to everyone but, on the other hand, I don't hide it either. I am a mother, I had a son. I felt today that it was appropriate that I tell those parents what had happened to me before they marched into Emily and made exactly the same mistake my parents made…'

'A lot of parents do.'

'Well, hopefully Emily's parents shan't now,' Marnie said. 'I certainly didn't tell them to make you feel uncomfortable.'

'They didn't take it well, then?' Harry asked. 'Your parents?'

'No.' Marnie hesitated. Normally she'd add something sharp here, like, 'Just because you know about it doesn't mean that I want to discuss it.' Except today, right now, she did. Maybe it was because Harry, given he had lost his wife, surely knew grief. Or maybe it was just with Declan's birthday coming up and Ronan hinting that her mother was upset, it had all been brought to the surface.

Then she looked up to his green eyes that were waiting patiently and realised that maybe it was just because it was Harry. 'They're very strict,' Marnie said. 'Or rather they were when we were younger. My mum went crazy when she found out. She said that it would kill my granny and my father...' She gave a tight smile. 'Though not till he'd killed the baby's father.' Marnie closed her eyes at the weary memory of that time. 'All the usual stuff.'

'Like?'

'I'm sure you can guess.' Marnie gave a tight shrug. 'She also made it very clear that she didn't think I should keep my baby. Anyway, a few months later when my son was on the neonatal unit, the person I wanted was my mum but at the same time I didn't want her. We can't discuss it, even now.'

'Have you tried?'

'Nope.' Marnie shook her head. 'And I won't be trying either.' She looked at Harry. 'It couldn't end nicely.' Marnie felt uncomfortable now; the only person she really discussed Declan with was her friend Siobhan and, feeling she'd said more than enough, Marnie changed the subject. 'I'm just very glad that Emily's father didn't march in and vent his spleen. She had a big abruption, and she could start bleeding again any time soon,' Marnie said. 'That baby's far from safe.' She wanted to stop talking about it, she wanted to just end the conversation, to dismiss Harry and get on with her day, except Marnie felt her nose redden and Harry saw a flash of tears in her eyes.

'Marnie...' Harry was struggling for words—he was used to death, both personally and professionally, and had it been anyone else he'd have stood, gone over, but it was Marnie, and he didn't. Not because he didn't want to, more because of how much he did.

'It's fine.' Marnie filled the silence. 'I'm fine. It was all just a bit too close to home.' She blew out a breath. 'It's his birthday coming up.'

'Look, do you want to...?' Harry's voice trailed off as there was a knock at the door.

'Matthew!' Harry noticed that she flushed a little as a rather well-dressed man entered. 'What are you doing here?' Marnie asked.

'I had a client nearby,' Matthew said. 'I thought I might see if you were free for lunch. Oh, and I wanted to tell you in person that I got the tickets.' He handed an envelope to Marnie. 'Opening night, don't ask me how I got them!'

'Oh!' Marnie's anger at having her workspace invaded was temporarily thwarted because, more than anything, she loved the ballet and the opening night had sold out the day the tickets had been released. 'Wow!'

'It might be better if you look after them,' Matthew said, not even bothering to introduce himself to Harry, who had already made up his mind that he didn't like him.

'I'll leave you to it,' Harry said, and walked out.

Harry wasn't sure if he was jealous of Marnie's freedom or just plain jealous—Harry had been very close to suggesting they leave the department and get lunch.

Stupid idea, Harry, he told himself. Those days were long gone—he kept things well away from work.

A moment or so later he looked up from a patient and saw them walking out of the department, Matthew sliding a hand around Marnie's waist.

He didn't like that and neither did Marnie—she wriggled out of Matthew's embrace and it was clear she was cross.

'Are you going to show me where you live?' Matthew asked as she got into his car and he started the engine.

'Sure,' Marnie said, her tongue firmly in her cheek.

'My brother Ronan is over for a couple of days. You can say hi if you like...'

'Maybe not, then.'

Sitting in a bayside café a little while later, Marnie told him that she was far from impressed.

'Why would you drop in on me at work?' Marnie asked.

'I told you—I was in the area and I wanted to give you the tickets for the ballet or I'd end up losing them. I'm going straight from here to the airport.'

Marnie refused to buy it. 'Until recently I lived a stone's throw from your office and I would never have dropped in on you!' She was angry, very angry—part of the loose arrangement they had was that there would be no popping in. She and Matthew went out now and then. They were social and, yes, they slept together, but they did not invade each other's lives and that was the way Marnie wanted it. 'Whatever possessed you?'

'Okay, okay,' Matthew said, deciding against suggesting that she call in sick this afternoon. 'I shan't stop by again.' He watched as Marnie's hand, which had just dipped her bread in oil, paused over the salt. 'I wouldn't want to disturb anything.'

'Excuse me?'

'You and your colleague looked very cosy.'

'We were talking about a patient!' Marnie so did not need this. 'He's got two children...' Marnie shook her head and then reached for her bag. 'I need to get back.'

They drove in silence. Marnie was still cross, not just that Matthew had dropped by at her work but cross with herself for all she had told Harry. Cross too that Matthew had interrupted them.

'The ballet will be great,' Matthew said, as he dropped her off. 'Get you back to civilisation.'

Far from being offended, she actually laughed. Maybe she did need a night of being spoilt, it might stop the constant thoughts about Declan's birthday.

And about Harry.

As she went to get a drink of water from the staff kitchen she was met by a very stony-faced Harry, who was rinsing his mug.

'Nice lunch?'

'Lovely, thanks.'

'Your boyfriend—?'

'Boyfriend?' Marnie rapidly interrupted. 'I'm thirty-one—I'm a bit old for boys.'

'Sorry.' Harry gave a wry grin. She was the most impossible person he had ever met, yet, for reasons of his own, which he didn't really want to examine, he ploughed on. 'Your partner, then?'

'Partner?' Marnie challenged him right there and then. She was sick of men and the different rules that applied to them, and Marnie told him so. Despite never gossiping herself, Marnie was very clued in and had heard all the rumours about Harry. 'Is that what you called your last nanny? Your partner, your girlfriend?' Harry let out a breath as Marnie continued, 'Or did you upgrade her title to your live-in lover?'

'I was just going to say he seemed nice.'

'Well, I'll let you know when I need your opinion.'

Marnie dived into work, refusing to go to her office because that would look like she was hiding. And why would she be hiding? There was nothing to feel embarrassed or awkward about—a friend had merely dropped in to take her to lunch.

It was just that Marnie didn't like her worlds colliding and, as the afternoon progressed, the tension seemed to increase. Near home time she glanced up and briefly caught sight of a very dark-looking Harry walking past, and she knew it wasn't just that Matthew had dropped by that was unsettling her.

It was Harry.

In a nice way, though.

There was a tiny flutter in her chest as she met his eyes and it was still fluttering as she looked away and tried to concentrate on what Kelly was calling out to her.

'Sorry?' She looked at Kelly.

'There's a guy on the phone for you,' Kelly repeated. 'He says it's personal.'

'I'll bet it is,' Harry muttered, but thankfully well out of earshot.

What the hell did Matthew want now? Marnie thought as she made her way over. Only it wasn't Matthew calling her at work and she saw Harry's jaw grit as she said another man's name.

'Ronan, what are you doing, phoning me at work?'

He wanted to take the receiver from her and replace it. He wanted to turn her round and tell her part of the reason for his dark mood.

He couldn't get her out of his mind.

CHAPTER SIX

HARRY REACHED FOR his jacket. It was ten to five and he was in no mood for *another* dose of salt to be rubbed into a very raw wound, and anyway he had to get to his parents to pick up the twins and inspect them for chickenpox.

Fun!

'Are you heading off?' Dr Vermont said, and Harry nodded.

'You're not in tomorrow?' Dr Vermont checked.

'I can't leave them with my parents for too long,' Harry said, and Dr Vermont nodded. He knew Harry's father's health wasn't brilliant and the twins were hard work at the best of times. By the time Harry had signed off on some paperwork, Marnie had gathered her bag and was walking briskly through the department, jangling her car keys.

'You're in a rush, Marnie,' Dr Vermont commented, because Marnie never usually left till well past six. 'Is everything okay?'

'I'll be back,' Marnie said. 'My brother just called and he's cut himself—his finger. I'm just going home to fetch him and bring him in.'

'I'll stay around to see him,' Dr Vermont said, and Marnie gave a grateful smile, though, in truth, it was a bit of a forced one because she desperately wanted Harry to offer to stay back. He was, as she was starting to find out, not just considered the best hand surgeon in the hospital but one of the top in the country.

Harry made no offer; instead, he joined her as she headed out.

She walked to the car park with him. Their footsteps were rapid and the atmosphere between them was tense but it was Harry who broke the strained silence. 'Do you think it's serious?'

'It's deep. I told him to make dinner and he couldn't find my tin-opener so he decided to use a knife...' She was waffling, stupidly feeling guilty for insisting that Ronan cook, but she was evading the real answer, not because she didn't want to tell Harry, more because she didn't want to think what it might mean to Ronan. 'He says it's bad.' Harry could hear the slight panic in her voice as she elaborated, 'I'm worried he might have cut a tendon.'

'You haven't even seen it yet.' Harry was practical.

'He plays the piano.' Marnie glanced at Harry. 'I mean—he plays it really well.' She closed her eyes for a second. If Ronan had indeed injured his tendon it was going to be a tough few months ahead for him, with no guarantee his hand would return to full dexterity.

'If he has injured his tendon, Dr Vermont will refer him to Stuart. He's on tonight and he's a great surgeon.'

She wanted Harry.

They were now at her car and, given how inflexible Marnie had been with his children, she was in absolutely no position to ask him a favour, except it was Ronan. For that reason, and that reason only, Marnie swallowed her pride and went to speak, but the words wouldn't come out. Harry watched as she ran one of those very beautiful hands through her dark hair as again she tried to swallow her pride.

For Ronan, Marnie told herself.

'If it needs doing, is there any chance of you repairing it tomorrow?' There were two spots of colour appearing on her pale cheeks. 'If Dr Vermont orders it to be elevated tonight, you could—'

'I'm not coming in tomorrow.'

'Oh, I thought you were on.'

'No.'

When Harry didn't elaborate, Marnie just nodded and got into her car. She loathed that she'd asked him but, more than that, she loathed that he'd said no.

When she got home, Marnie let herself in and Ronan called out to her. 'I'm in here.'

He was sitting on the floor of Marnie's bathroom with his hand wrapped in a towel and he was holding it up.

'You don't have a bath to sit on,' was the first thing he said, and Marnie managed a smile as, first things first, she washed her hands.

'It was the first thing I noticed about the place too.' Marnie knelt down beside him and gently pulled down his arm.

'Sorry about the towel.'

'Don't worry about it,' Marnie said.

'I made a mess in the kitchen.'

'Ronan, stop.' She unwrapped the towel and Marnie, who was very used to looking at injured fingers, surprised herself by feeling a bit sick when she examined Ronan's cut. Marnie blew out a breath as she saw the white of Ronan's partially severed tendon as he attempted to move his finger.

'Don't try to do anything for now,' Marnie said. 'I'll put a dressing on it and we'll get you to the hospital.'

She went to the kitchen and it was a bit of a mess with Ronan's blood, as he'd said. She reached for a glass and took two long drinks of water then refilled the glass.

It was ridiculous really, Marnie thought. There wasn't a single thing at work that made her feel faint but as soon as it was family, it was a different matter entirely.

She stood, remembering the nurses insisting she wait outside as they stuck another needle in Declan…

Not now!

Marnie tipped the water down the sink, got out her first-aid box and headed back to Ronan. She sorted out the wound, wrapping the injured finger in a saline dressing and bandaging it, then applying a sling, before she got him into the car and headed to the hospital.

'It's bad, isn't it?' Ronan asked, as Marnie concentrated on driving.

'I think you've done your tendon,' she admitted.

'That can be fixed, though, can't it?'

'Of course it can.' She glanced over and smiled but said nothing more just yet. Ronan's tendon could certainly be fixed but it would take a lot of time and patience to get back the function that Ronan had had.

She wished that Harry was on tonight.

The department was quiet and Marnie took Ronan straight through and into a cubicle, where she told him to lie down.

'I don't need to lie down,' he said, then changed his mind. He was tall and geeky and didn't try to hide it, and Marnie loved him for it. 'I do feel a bit sick.'

'I know,' Marnie said, because the phrase 'as white as a sheet' could have been coined just for Ronan—

Marnie was quite sure that had he not lain down when he had he would have passed out.

'Can a have a glass of water?'

'Nothing.' Marnie shook her head. 'You can't have anything till a doctor's seen it. Just wait there and I'll go and get you registered and then...' Her voice trailed off as the curtain opened and Harry walked in.

'Harry!' Marnie couldn't quite believe that he was here—especially since she'd seen him drive off.

Harry couldn't quite believe it either. He'd got five minutes down the road, feeling as guilty as hell for saying no to Marnie's brother, when his phone had rung with the news from his mother that Adam was coming out in spots.

Harry had pulled over and sat with his head in his hands, listening to the sound of the traffic whizzing past.

Of course, if Adam had them, then Charlotte would get them soon.

Something had to give and at that moment it did.

Adam was fine when Harry rang back—he was the centre of attention for once when usually it was Charlotte.

'He's tired, though,' his mum explained. 'I was just going to put him to bed. Why don't you stay here tonight? It would be a shame to wake him.'

Harry hesitated. He had been about to say yes, but at the last moment he asked his aging parents for yet another favour.

For the last time.

Sure, he'd need them in the future, Harry didn't doubt that, but the madness had to stop and so he had ended it.

'Marnie.' He gave her a tight smile and then aimed a much nicer one at Ronan. 'So, I hear that you've cut your finger, cooking.' Harry helped Ronan out of the sling and when he saw the neat dressing he made a wry joke about Ronan's big sister having a fully equipped first-aid box.

'Yeah, well, she might have a well-equipped first-aid box but she doesn't have a tin-opener,' Ronan said, as Harry washed his hands and put on some gloves while Marnie removed the dressing.

'I do have tin-opener,' Marnie scolded. 'Just because Mum keeps hers in the second drawer, you didn't think to look in the third.'

Harry grinned to himself at the good-natured banter between brother and sister and then he came over and carefully examined the wound as well as testing for sensation in Adam's finger. 'You're a pianist, Marnie tells me?'

'I'm a computer programmer,' Ronan said.

'Well, you'd need your fingers working for that...' Harry opened a needle and checked Ronan's sensation more thoroughly as Marnie stood wondering if Harry was thinking he'd been brought in under false pretences.

'He's a very good pianist,' Marnie said. 'I didn't mean to make it sound like he was a maestro.'

'You didn't,' Harry said. He looked at Ronan. 'I'm sure you've realised that this injury is more than just a straightforward cut that can simply be stitched.'

'I pretty much knew straight away,' Ronan said. 'Will I still be able to play?' he asked, and Marnie found she was holding her breath as Harry dealt with the issue that she hadn't been able to talk about during the journey to the hospital. 'I mean, will I still be able to play at the level I was?'

'First I have to do my part,' Harry said, 'then the rest is going to be up to you.' Harry was honest. 'You'll be in a splint afterwards and looking at a lot of hand therapy. It's early days yet. For now we have to repair it and then see where we're at.'

'Harry's an amazing hand surgeon,' Marnie said. 'You couldn't be in better hands.'

'Excuse the pun,' Harry said, and Ronan gave a pale smile, then Harry went through more of what Ronan could expect. He was very calming—even as he discussed the extensive rehabilitation ahead. 'Right, we'll get you around to our minor theatre. The tendon's still partially intact so I'll be able to do it under a block, but first I need to go and get something to eat as it might take a while.'

'Can I have a drink?' Ronan asked.

'Sorry,' Harry said with a brief smile. 'That was cruel of me. No, you can't have anything in case you do end up needing a general anaesthetic.'

'You're doing him tonight?' Marnie checked.

'I told you I was!' There was a slight edge of irritation to Harry's voice when he addressed Marnie, which he quickly fought to check. 'I'm not available tomorrow and the sooner that it's repaired the better.'

'I can assist.'

Harry rolled his eyes. 'Have you looked in the mirror?' Marnie hadn't. 'Even your lips are white. I'll ask Kelly.'

Kelly came in and introduced herself to Ronan and Marnie excused herself as Kelly said she was going to get him into a gown and prepared for Theatre.

'I'll be waiting in my office,' Marnie said, but of course it didn't end there because Kelly was asking about Ronan's next of kin. 'I should ring Mum and tell her.'

'Not tonight.' Ronan shook his head. 'Please, Marnie, can that wait till tomorrow?'

Marnie was only too pleased to agree.

She gave Ronan a brief cuddle and then headed to the kitchen for another glass of water, where she found Harry feeding bread into the toaster.

'Thank you for coming back to do this.'

'It's fine,' Harry said.

'What about the children?'

'Charlotte and Adam are staying the night at my parents'. I'm going to get them tomorrow.'

'I feel awful…'

'Well, don't. You were right not to want Adam hanging around the department—he has got chickenpox.'

'Oh, no,' Marnie said. 'I feel terrible that he doesn't have you tonight.'

The toast popped up and Harry started buttering it but he did turn and speak at the same time. 'Marnie, it's my job—it's what I do. It's what I've been *trying* to do since Jill died. I can't count the times I called Jill and said someone had come in and that I needed to be here…'

'It's appreciated.'

'Good. I am the best hand surgeon in this hospital. I'd want me for this.'

'I'd want you to,' Marnie said, and from nowhere, absolutely from nowhere, a blush spread over her cheeks and, given how pale she had been, there was no chance of hiding it. 'I meant—'

'It's fine.

The strangest thing was, as the colour soared up her cheeks, Harry, who never blushed, thought that he might be as well.

Or was it just terribly warm?

'The thing is—' Marnie started, but Harry interrupted.

'Right, now I would just like ten minutes' peace before I go and do surgery,' Harry said, and, taking his toasted sandwich, he stalked off to his office rather than the staffroom, but there was no peace to be had there either.

There was an inbox that was so full it spilled over the edges and he daren't check his emails because he'd need a week to get them clear.

Harry ate his sandwich then changed into scrubs and headed into the minor theatre where Ronan lay, chatting with Kelly, who was setting up for the operation.

'I was just telling Ronan that he's got his sister's hands.' Kelly smiled.

'I don't remember Marnie's being quite so hairy,' Harry said, as he put in the nerve block that would ensure Ronan couldn't feel anything during surgery. 'Your accent isn't as strong as Marnie's. Though I guess you were much younger when you came to Melbourne.'

'We came to Perth first,' Ronan told him, and it wasn't, Harry noted, just Ronan's hands that were similar to Marnie's—he could talk for Ireland too. 'But Dad got transferred to Melbourne a couple of years later. I don't really remember Perth. I think I remember more about Ireland, though I'm not sure if it's from going back or Mum talking about it. I've been back twice now, though Marnie goes back far more often. She misses it like crazy.'

Harry looked up. 'Didn't she want to emigrate?'

'No,' Roman said. 'Though she didn't want to leave Perth either. She always said the moment she turned eighteen and she had her own passport she'd be straight back to Ireland, but she got into nursing…' Ronan didn't continue.

He didn't have to.

Harry pretty much knew what had happened from there. As he waited for the block to take effect, he spent a moment thinking about Marnie.

Harry's heart seemed to constrict for a moment.

No wonder she was so tough, she'd had to learn how to be.

He checked each finger in turn, making sure that the anaesthetic had taken full effect before starting.

It was a very intricate operation, which required Harry to wear magnifying glasses and to focus extremely hard, but every now and then Kelly would take his glasses off and he would sit up straight for a moment and take a very brief break. Sometimes he found himself listening to Ronan and Kelly talking, mostly about music and computers, but now and then the conversation drifted to Marnie.

'I fight all the time with my sister,' Kelly was saying.

'It's not worth fighting with Marnie,' Ronan said. 'It's her way or the highway.'

Ten years older than Ronan, Marnie had, it would seem, been a second mum more than a sister to him.

Funny that he found out more about Marnie during a sixty-minute operation than he had in all the time he'd worked alongside her.

'You're done,' Harry said, finishing off the splint. 'For tonight you'll stay in and we'll keep it elevated. You'll be given analgesics as it's going to be painful as sensation starts to return and I want to start you on antibiotics. The last thing we want is an infection.'

'Harry will come in and see you tomorrow,' Kelly said, 'and then you'll probably be discharged home.'

'Actually, I'm off tomorrow,' Harry said. 'It will be Dr Vermont and then there will be follow-ups in the hand clinic and a referral to the hand therapist.' He really couldn't tell Kelly and Ronan his news before he'd told Dr Vermont.

And Marnie too.

'Take care,' Harry settled for instead.

He had a drink before heading into Marnie's office, and when he got there she was sitting with her head in her hands, just as he had in the car earlier, as if bracing herself for the news that her brother had died!

'It's a tendon!' Harry said.

'I know.' Marnie looked up and there was a grimace on her face as she tried to force a smile. 'I just came off the phone to my mother—you wouldn't believe me if I told you how difficult that conversation was. She actually rang me and I caved and told her about Ronan's accident.'

'Oh.' Harry was surprised. He'd got the impression they barely spoke. 'I thought you didn't…' Harry halted. It was none of his business.

'We may not talk about certain things,' Marnie said, 'but, as difficult as they can be, I love my parents very much.' Marnie lifted her eyes to the ceiling. 'Ronan's accident is all my fault.'

'Of course it is,' Harry said calmly.

'If she woke up tomorrow and the sky was purple, she'd be on the phone, blaming me.'

'Well, if you'd just kept the tin-opener in the second drawer, all this could have been avoided.' Harry wagged his finger and somehow made her smile, and then she looked away because Harry was usually in a suit. She didn't think she'd seen so much of his skin before, at least, not this close up. His arms were very long but muscular too, and she could see just a smattering of chest hair when Marnie was rather more used to smooth. He looked tired yet there was a certain air of elation to him that Marnie didn't quite understand.

'I've managed to convince her to not visit till tomorrow, it would be after ten before she got here. How did the repair go?'

'Very well,' Harry said. 'Kelly will be bringing him round to the obs ward soon....' His voice trailed off as his pager went and Harry read the message, then asked if he could use her phone.

'Sure.'

'Hi, Mum,' Harry said. 'Yes, sorry about that, it took a bit longer than I thought. Put him on.' Marnie tried to look away as he chatted to Adam but her eyes kept drifting towards him.

To think she'd expected him to have a bit of a paunch by now—he had a very flat stomach and very muscular legs and, as he sat on the edge of her desk as he spoke, Marnie could see the hair on his arms.

He was, as if Marnie didn't already know, very, very beautiful.

Dangerous too.

Dangerous, because Marnie rarely opened up to anyone, yet with Harry she did too easily. Even the brief conversation about her phone call with her mother was far more than she would usually share and Marnie's foot tapped, with tension rather than impatience, as Harry spoke on.

She wanted to get away from him.

She wanted to go home, just so she could give herself a good talking to.

After speaking to Adam, he chatted at length to Charlotte, though he could see Marnie's foot tapping in mid-air out of the corner of his eye, but then she stood and went and stared out of the window as Harry laughed and talked on. 'What do you mean, it's not fair?' He spoke a little while longer and then said goodnight and put down the phone.

'Charlotte's jealous that Adam has got chickenpox,' Harry said to Marnie, who was still looking out of the window. He watched her shoulders move in a small laugh and then wretched guilt at keeping him from his children caught up and Marnie turned her head.

'Say it,' Marnie challenged, her blue eyes glittering.

'Say what?' Harry frowned.

'Go on,' Marnie insisted. 'Say whatever's on your mind.'

Harry gave a wry grin. 'Such as…'

'It's different when it's you or your family,' Marnie offered, turning to face him.

'That's not what's on my mind.'

'Hypocrite, then?' Marnie suggested.

'No…' He was walking towards her.

'Just say it.'

'You're quite sure?' Harry said, and it was at that moment exactly that she realised that Harry had something else on his mind, something very similar to what was on hers as she saw the burn of arousal in his eyes. 'You're quite sure that you want me to say what's on my mind?'

She looked at him properly then, saw the Harry she hadn't seen in a very long time. There was an energy to him that had been missing, an energy that she hadn't seen since a certain night in the doctors' mess when he'd asked why she was leaving so soon—only this time it was potent.

If he'd been on the other side of the desk, she might have had a chance to deny him. Might have been able to rein in common sense and come up with some witty retort that would end things before they were started.

Except he was standing in front of her. She could smell the lust, the want, the need, and it was intoxicating and, quite simply, Marnie couldn't resist. One small nod was all the affirmation needed for Harry to tell his truth.

'I want you.'

His mouth came down and crushed Marnie's. He was so tall he had to, not just stoop but almost lift her to exert the pressure that this kiss demanded.

Marnie was no stranger to lust but she'd never felt it as ferociously or as deliciously as this.

Every snap, every snarl, every flirt, every tease was now being paid back tenfold by the probe of his tongue and the roaming of his hands.

Or was it her hands? One was in his hair, messing it to the way she had first seen it, the other moving down over his arm, but only so she could force a space to get to his back and to the taut buttocks she had admired from behind on far too many occasions.

It was lust uninterrupted, Marnie for once out of control, and she liked it.

'I remember you now...' He was opening the buttons to her navy dress and not for a moment did she think of halting him. Whatever was wrong in the world, this was the antidote and for now, this moment, they celebrated their discovery. 'Harry...' She could feel his arousal pressed into her; one hand was lifting her dress and he moaned into her mouth as he felt her soft thigh. As he slipped his hand higher, it was Marnie who moaned.

'Not here...' Marnie pulled back but her words were contrary to her actions; she was kissing his face, her hands lifting his top just to get to his skin, just to bury her mouth in his salty chest and taste him. 'Not here...'

Marnie moaned again, and Harry almost came as he looked down at her licking her lips. 'Harry.' She was wrestling for control. Hell, she was the nurse unit manager, her mother could have changed her mind and arrived any minute, Kelly could knock at the door...

'I don't get involved with anyone at work.'

'Not a problem.' Harry turned the lock on her door and then picked her up and lifted her over to the desk. 'I just resigned.'

CHAPTER SEVEN

'YOU WHAT?'

He was back to her mouth but now Marnie understood his earlier elation.

'Harry? You can't.'

'I already have.' He looked down at her breasts, pale in their bra, and he wanted to bury his face in them, to simply forget, but he knew then that the moment was over and, still breathless, still hard, still wanting, he did the right thing and started to do the buttons up.

Yes, it had been about escape, Marnie realised, for a man who wasn't thinking particularly straight, and it was time for her to steer things towards reason.

'Harry…' She was struggling to get her breath back too. His groin was still leaning into hers, her body still tingling and aroused, and it would be so much easier to dive back to his mouth, but instead she offered no resistance as he straightened up. In fact, she shivered a little at the coolness when he was gone.

'I apologise.'

'For what?' Marnie attempted to laugh it off. 'I didn't notice me doing much resisting, but I don't think a quick shag on the office desk is going to solve things.'

He smiled at her directness. 'I don't think anything

is going to solve things,' he admitted. 'Might be nice to give it a try, though.'

Marnie retied her hair and brushed her dress down then unlocked the door. 'As if the person on the other side wouldn't know what was going on!'

Harry wanted to pull her down to his lap, perhaps take it more slowly this time, take her home even—after all, he had the house to himself. He didn't want to think about what he had done—the handing-in-the-notice part, not the Marnie part. He'd love to think more about that! No, it was handing in his notice. His ten-past-five phone call to Admin that he didn't want to examine, but Marnie refused to let it drop.

'You love your job, Harry.'

'I love it when I get to do it,' Harry said.

'So what are you going to do?'

'Go private,' Harry said. 'Hand surgery...'

'Will it be enough?' Marnie asked. 'Harry, you love this place...'

'I love my children more,' Harry said. 'There will still be accident and emergency departments needing a consultant in a few years' time—right now the children need some stability.'

'You can give them that,' Marnie said, horrified to think of the department without him. Harry and Dr Vermont were the lynchpins of the place. Yes, there were new doctors starting but they needed guidance.

'It's not up for discussion,' Harry said. 'The deed is done.'

'How long's your notice?'

'Two weeks,' Harry said, 'but I'm not working it. I'm taking parental leave to look after the children.'

'That's it?' Marnie said, understanding more and

more where the emotion of the night had come from. Harry really was leaving the place.

'That's it,' Harry said. 'There will probably be a leaving do in a couple of weeks, which I'll do my best to get to—' his voice was wry '—providing I can get a babysitter.'

'Harry—'

'Leave it.'

Sex would have been so much easier.

Harry hadn't cried since the night before he'd lost Jill. He hadn't been able to, there had been two bewildered twins to look after and Jill's shocked parents as well as his own—all his grieving had been done on the ICU ward before the machines had been turned off, yet, on this day, he was precariously close to breaking down.

He loved his job—an A and E consultant was all he had ever wanted to be and it was killing him to walk away.

Yet it was impossible to stay.

'Come home with me?' he said, looking at her very full mouth.

She could feel his eyes there, wanted again the weight of his kiss, but not like this…

'Harry, if I come home with you, it will be to talk some sense into you.'

'You can talk sense into me over dinner.'

She was tempted, so tempted, and that was the problem.

She wanted dinner with Harry, and bed, and she wanted to know so much more about him. She looked into eyes that were as come hither as they had been all those years ago, only now it would be so terribly easy to say yes.

Dinner with Harry would be lovely.

Bed even better.

There was just one little problem.

Make that two.

How could she best put it?

'I'm busy tonight, Harry,' Marnie said. 'What about Saturday?'

It hit Harry where she had intended to—right below the belt. Ardour faded as Marnie flexed the freedom muscle she guarded so fiercely. It would take a whole lot more than the occasional night off, babysitter permitting, to lure Marnie.

'Saturday might be a problem.'

Yes, she'd rather thought that it might.

'I'm going to go,' Harry said, but Marnie hadn't finished discussing her favourite subject.

Work.

'Harry, you're rushing into this decision—'

'I'm not rushing into anything,' Harry interrupted. 'If anything, this is long overdue. I'll come in and say goodbye to everyone when the time's right, but now I need to take care of my kids.'

He left her in the office, stunned from the news, from his kiss, from the sudden absence of Harry.

He wanted his last walk through *his* department alone.

''Night, Harry,' Kelly called.

''Night,' Harry called back. 'Thanks for your help with Ronan.'

He nodded to Helen, the locum who was covering for tonight, and, yes, the place was going to struggle, but it would soon move on. Juan would be back and Dr Cooper would start.

He'd just miss it so much.

* * *

Dr Vermont broke the news to the staff the next morning.

'We all know what a struggle it's been for Harry since Jill died. It's not an easy decision to make but for Harry it must have been the right one.'

Marnie felt terrible—she kept beating herself up, wondering if she'd just been a bit more flexible the outcome might have been different. And, on top of all that, over and over she kept remembering the steamy kiss they had shared. Yes, she fancied Harry, but the impact of him close up had shaken her more than she had thought it would. Still, she didn't have much time to dwell on it. As the staff spilled out of the staffroom, all talking about the news of Harry's sudden departure, Marnie walked straight into her parents.

'Mum!' Marnie gave her mother a smile and a kiss.

'What was he doing, using a knife to open a can?' Maureen accused.

'You can't blame Marnie for this.' Ronan laughed and tried to sit up with one hand attached to a pole as Dr Vermont came over to visit the patients in the obs ward.

'Mr Johnson,' Dr Vermont said, and Marnie smothered a smile as her father stepped forward, because Dr Vermont was speaking to Ronan. 'I hear everything went very well last night.' Marnie took down Ronan's hand from the pole and Dr Vermont checked the colour and sensation in the tip of Ronan's heavily splinted finger. He asked Ronan to try and move the finger and Marnie watched with relief as the pink tip lifted just a little.

'You can feel this?' Dr Vermont checked as Ronan closed his eyes.

'Yes.'

Marnie let out a breath and then smiled as Ronan again said he could feel the touch of the needle as Dr Vermont checked the other side.

'It's doing everything it should,' Dr Vermont said. 'I'll see you in two days and then...' He hesitated as he looked at the address on the admission notes. 'Do you do want to be followed up here?' Dr Vermont checked. 'I see that you live quite a distance away.'

'Here would be great,' Ronan said. 'I can catch up with Marnie when I have an appointment.'

'It's the only way you'll get to see her,' Maureen Johnson muttered, and Marnie chose not to respond to her mother's barb and stayed silent as Dr Vermont spoke to Kelly. 'Could you schedule in some hand appointments for Mr Johnson?' he asked, and then turned to Ronan. 'If we book the next couple in, at least you'll know what you're doing.'

He gave a few more instructions and then moved on to the next bed.

'You can get dressed,' Marnie said to her brother a little while later when Kelly had come off the phone.

'I'll give him a hand,' Kelly said, as she pulled the curtains around the bed. 'I've made the appointments. We'll see you the day after tomorrow and then again on the twenty-third. Is that okay?'

Ronan looked up at his sister, but thankfully the curtain swished past and Marnie had a second to collect herself before she answered for him.

'The twenty-third's fine,' Marnie said, and deliberately didn't look at her mum as the one date they all dreaded was, for the first time in a very long time, mentioned.

Trust the Irish to not make a fuss when it mattered!

CHAPTER EIGHT

'THIS TOO WILL pass,' Dr Vermont said. 'It's my favourite saying and one I've used often over the years working in this place.'

It was two in the morning and Marnie was on her first night shift at Bayside. It had been difficult logistically without Harry as they struggled to cover the department but, more than logistics, he was sorely missed by everyone, including Marnie.

Especially Marnie.

She was missing him on a whole different level, though—the flirting, the teasing, just the fun of having someone as shamelessly male as Harry around.

Not that she told that to Dr Vermont, of course. They were going through the doctors' roster for the next couple of weeks and trying to cover the gaps as they ate Marnie's chicken and mango salad that she had brought in from home.

'I've been through staff shortages, work to rule, the whole lot,' Dr Vermont continued. 'And, though it feels like it will never end, invariably it does. It will all get sorted, and I'll say it again—this is not your fault.'

Dr Vermont was lovely and extremely practical when Marnie had confessed what was on her mind.

'Even if you had let Charlotte, or was it Adam, lie on the sofa, this still would have happened.'

'I was trying to make things easier for him,' Marnie admitted. 'I know I looked like I was being mean when I told him to go home a couple of times but I was trying to show him that he wasn't completely indispensable...'

Dr Vermont laughed. 'Well, you did!'

'I know.' Marnie ran a worried hand over her forehead. 'I was trying to prove to him that we could call the trauma team or the medics, that it didn't have to all fall to him,' Marnie explained. 'I just wish that I'd handled things a little differently. I wish—'

'Marnie,' Dr Vermont interrupted, 'Harry has been struggling to find balance between work and home since Jill died. I honestly don't know how he's managed to do this job for so long without a partner. Marjorie, my wife, managed to have a career and raise our family, but we had a lot of support too. Harry's sister and parents all live a couple of hours away.'

Dr Vermont thought for a moment. 'I could not have done this job and raised a family without Marjorie. Even when the place is fully covered you can still expect to be called in. I can't tell you how many nights I've been on take and yet I've still rung Harry to come in to give an opinion, or there's been a multiple trauma and another pair of hands has been needed. Marjorie was more than used to it—long before coffee machines were around she made sure there was a flask of coffee by my bed so that I could have a drink as I drove in.' He smiled at the memory and so did Marnie. 'What I'm trying to explain...'

His voice trailed off and Marnie looked up from her salad, waiting for him to continue. 'Dr Vermont?' Marnie stood. For a bizarre, still hopeful, second, she hoped that he might have fallen asleep in mid-sentence, but even as she called his name again, Marnie knew what was happening. As she dropped her salad and raced around her desk, he took a couple of laboured breaths and she watched as Dr Vermont's skin tinged to grey and he let out an ominous gurgle.

'Dr Vermont!' Marnie shouted, as she tried to locate a carotid pulse. Her mind was in twenty places—she held onto his shoulder as he toppled forward and Marnie knew she couldn't get to the phone or door without him falling to the floor.

'Can I have some help?' Marnie shouted, trying to break his fall and kick the chair away at the same time, but no one was answering. 'Can someone…?' She laid Dr Vermont on the floor and raced to open the door, shouting loudly for help as she grabbed the phone from her desk.

Summon help, the nursing part of her brain told her, yet she wanted to start compressions. Marnie put out a crash call, explaining to the startled switchboard operator that she had to be specific. 'Code red, Emergency Department, in the nurse unit manager's office.' She was shouting, Marnie realised, when usually she was calm. 'Make sure you say that.'

She started compressions as the intercom crackled into life. But, alerted by her shouting, Clive, the night porter, came running.

'Oh, no…' he moaned, but he knew, without Marnie telling him, exactly what to do.

'I'll get help.'

'Get the crash trolley as well,' Marnie called, as she carried on with the compressions.

There was nothing emergency staff dreaded more

than family or friends being brought in, but to have a colleague suddenly collapse at work was truly awful.

The staff came running and in no time Marnie's office looked more like the resuscitation room. Eric, the on-call cardiologist, arrived first. His shocked expression as he saw Dr Vermont lying on the floor, his shirt open, his glasses off, was one Marnie would never forget.

Abby was trying not to cry as she charged the defibrillator and Marnie could see the resident's hand shaking as he delivered yet another shock.

'Nothing.'

'We need to get him to Resuscitation,' the cardiologist said. He was breathless from running but helped to lift Dr Vermont onto the trolley that Clive had brought in. They sped Dr Vermont through the department and the resuscitation continued en route—Marnie kneeling on the trolley to continue the compressions as Abby pushed oxygen in with an Ambu bag.

The night supervisor came, as she often did when an emergency page had been put out, but she too had run just a little harder when she had heard the strange alert.

'It's Dr Vermont,' Marnie said, stepping down as Eric took over the compressions, frantically trying to pump the medications through Dr Vermont's system in the hope the next shock would have some effect.

It didn't.

'We need to let his wife know,' the night supervisor said as the team grimly worked on.

Marnie's hands were shaking as she went through the contact sheets, dreading the thought of calling Mrs Vermont in the middle of the night to tell her that her husband was critically ill.

'Get Harry to call her,' Eric shouted over. 'Has he been told what's going on?'

'Harry no longer works here,' Marnie said, and Eric shot her a wide-eyed look.

'I can guarantee Harry would want to be the one to tell her,' Eric said.

'Even if he's on leave, Harry needs to be informed,' the night supervisor said. 'Right now the emergency department doesn't have a consultant.'

Harry didn't deliberately not pick up the first time the phone rang. He was putting anti-itch cream on a miserable Adam, who had woken at one a.m. and couldn't get back to sleep.

'So much for a mild dose,' Harry said to his son. Apparently you could get a mild dose after a child had been immunised. Harry had found all the immunisation records and had spent half an hour looking at Jill's handwriting—she had recorded every milestone, every little detail of their little lives and, yes, bang on the suggested dates, Charlotte and Adam had received their immunisations.

Adam getting chickenpox was just another thing that had gone wrong on top of another thing that had gone wrong, Harry was thinking when the phone rang.

Would they not just let him leave? Harry sighed, letting it ring out, but then, worried it might be his parents, he tucked Adam in and went and checked the machine.

'Harry, it's Marnie, could you call me back at work please?' He could hear the strain in her voice. 'I'm sorry to call you but it is an emergency.'

What the hell was he supposed to do from here? Harry thought, picking up the phone when it rang again.

'Harry, it's Marnie.'

'Marnie, I've got a child who's sick—'

'Harry, please,' Marnie broke in. 'I have some very difficult news to tell you.' Harry heard she was struggling and the line went very quiet for a moment before he spoke.

'Go on.'

'Dr Vermont collapsed a short while ago,' Marnie said, and she heard his sharp intake of breath as she spoke on. 'He's in full cardiac arrest.'

'Oh, no.'

'We're doing everything we can but I have to tell you, Harry...' She glanced over, they were still going but more and more it was looking hopeless. 'It doesn't look good at all.'

'Is Marjorie there?'

'It's only just happened,' Marnie said. 'I was just away to inform her when Eric said that you'd want to know and perhaps be the one to tell her.'

Harry sat on the edge of his bed and he remembered the kindness the Vermonts had shown him; he remembered all they had done for him when Jill's accident had happened, and, yes, it was right that he be the one to tell Marjorie.

'I've got the twins...' He didn't want to wake them up and drag them out; he didn't want that for them but sometimes, no matter how inconvenient, certain things just had to be done. There was no choice—the doctor in charge of the department was critically ill, no doubt the staff were distraught and, given Dr Vermont had given more than thirty years of his life to the place, certainly his wife deserved to hear it from him. 'I'll ring her now and then I'll pick her up,' Harry said. 'Marnie, I'll have to bring the twins in.'

There was no argument this time.

And no little barbs either.

It was all too sad.

'Adam's infectious, probably Charlotte is too,' Harry said.

'So were half the patients that came through tonight,' Marnie said. 'The observation ward is empty, I'll make up two beds and close it off for further admissions.' Her voice was back to practical and it helped because Harry felt as though the whole pack of cards was falling again, just as he'd almost rebuilt it.

'Do you need Marjorie's number?' Marnie asked.

Of course, he already had it.

Harry rang off and he'd have loved to gather his thoughts for a moment but instead he dressed and then woke the twins and put them into their dressing gowns.

'I'm sorry, guys,' he said as he carried them down the stairs and out into the night, 'but Dr Vermont is very sick and we need to go and get Marjorie so that she can be with him.'

Only when they were strapped in and already nearly back to sleep did Harry stand in the driveway and call Marjorie.

He told her what was happening as best he could, and of course he knew Marjorie well, knew she would be dressing as they spoke and about to get into her car and fly through the night to be beside the man she had been married to for forty years.

'I'm on my way now, Marjorie,' Harry said. 'I'll be there in a few minutes.'

He was—Marjorie was out on the street and she was trying not to cry as she climbed in

'You shouldn't have brought the children out,' Marjorie told him. 'I could have got there myself.'

Except her knees were bobbing up and down as she

tried to sit still, the adrenaline coursing through her as the enormity of what was happening started to take hold. 'Is he....?' She couldn't even say it. 'I'd rather know now.'

'They were working on him when I last spoke to the hospital,' Harry said.

Harry didn't know if it was a good sign or bad when he saw Abby and Marnie waiting for them in the ambulance area.

'There's half the hospital in with Dr Vermont,' Marnie said as Harry came around and briefly pulled her aside. 'Abby said that twins would know her.'

'How is he?'

'We're just waiting for Marjorie,' Marnie said, taking a sleepy Charlotte as Abby carried Adam, freeing Harry to help Marjorie into the department.

Harry knew from her voice and words that they were just keeping things going till Marjorie arrived.

'Hello.' Marnie felt the sleepy weight of Charlotte stir in her arms as she lowered her onto a bed. 'Daddy's just in with a patient; he said to make sure you had a comfy bed. I'm Marnie.'

'I know,' Charlotte said, and turned over and went back to sleep.

Adam was a bit tearful and asked where his dad was. 'I'm here, Adam.' Harry came in at that moment. 'You can go back to sleep.'

'How's Dr Vermont?'

'He's not well at all,' Harry said, 'but Marjorie's with him so that's good. You just turn over and go to sleep and I'll let you know more in the morning.'

Marnie felt a swallow in her throat at the disruption to their little lives. Saw how, with barely a murmur of protest, Adam did as he was told and rolled over.

'What's happening round there?' Marnie asked once they had moved away from the sleeping twins.

'Marjorie told them to stop.' Harry's voice wavered and Marnie watched as he struggled to keep it together. After all, less than half an hour ago he'd been putting cream on Adam's spots.

He went over to Abby, who was sitting at the desk, crying quietly, and put a hand on her shoulder, but he spoke to Marnie. 'I think you might want to put the ambulances on diversion—a lot of the staff are going to be really upset.'

'Sure.' Marnie nodded. 'I've arranged for a couple of nurses to come down from the wards to help out.'

'Good. Are you okay?' Harry asked.

'I'll be fine,' Marnie said, though she could feel tears stinging at the back of her nose, but, really, it wasn't her place to be upset. She'd only known Dr Vermont a short while and, more importantly than that, she was the manager. Like Harry, tonight really wasn't about her—it was about doing their best for Dr Vermont and his family and the colleagues who would miss him so much.

'Who found him?' Harry asked. 'Eric said that he collapsed in his office.'

'We were in my office,' Marnie corrected. 'We were having supper and talking…' She pressed her fingers into her eyes for a brief moment and then recovered. 'He just stopped talking in mid-sentence.'

'You might need to speak to Marjorie,' Harry said, as he headed back out there. 'She might want to hear what happened from you.'

Marnie nodded. 'Harry!' She called him back. 'I don't know his first name.'

'Gregory,' Harry said. 'Gregory Vermont.'

* * *

Marjorie was as lovely as Dr Vermont had been and, though devastated, she was very stoic too.

'He spoke very highly of you,' Marjorie said when she'd been in to see her husband and was sitting down in his office, which was filled not just with his many certificates but with photos of his family too. 'He said you were going to bring a bit of order to the place...' She swallowed. 'Harry said that you were with him when it happened?'

'We were in my office,' Marnie said. 'We were having our supper break and talking about...' She glanced at Harry, who filled in for her.

'The Harry problem?'

'The staff issues,' Marnie said. 'He was actually talking about you. How you'd managed to have a career but how he couldn't have been an emergency doctor without all your support.' There was a flash of tears in Marnie's eyes as she recalled the conversation, such a simple one at the time but it was so much more meaningful now. Marjorie gave a grateful smile as Marnie recalled Dr Vermont's final moments, gave her the comfort of knowing he had been speaking about his wife and a marriage that had so clearly worked.

'He was telling me how you used to keep a flask of coffee by the bedside. Then he just stopped speaking, Marjorie,' Marnie said. 'There was no pain, no discomfort, I promise you that. For a moment I honestly thought that he'd fallen asleep...'

She heard a sniff and looked over. It was Harry. He'd been holding Marjorie's hand but now it was more that she was holding his.

'He thought the world of you,' Marjorie said to Harry, and Marnie watched as Harry nodded.

She felt as if she was glimpsing something incredibly private as, just for a moment, Harry gave in to his grief and screwed up his face, trying and failing not to weep.

'When you came to do your residency, he said what a great emergency doctor you'd make,' Marjorie said, and Harry nodded again but pulled himself together, when perhaps he didn't have to. Dr Vermont and Marjorie were, Marnie was fast realising, so much more than a colleague and his wife to Harry. They clearly went back years.

Marjorie went to sit with her husband again and to speak with her family, who were starting to arrive.

It was a wretched night and looked no better by morning. Marnie had placed the department on by-pass so that no ambulances were bringing patients in, though the walking wounded still trickled in. There were a couple of ward nurses helping out and one of the surgeons had come down to assist too. The nursing staff had known Dr Vermont for a lot longer than she had and needed each other more than they needed her, so Marnie took herself around to the observation ward and sat with the twins. She went through the doctors' rosters and tried to work out how the department could possibly work without even one senior doctor.

'Are you okay?' Harry came in a little later to check on the twins. He didn't want to wake them again and also wanted to be there to tell the day staff the sad news himself when they started to arrive.

'Of course.' Marnie nodded. 'You?'

'I just can't take it in,' Harry admitted, sitting down at the desk beside her and talking in a low voice so as not to disturb the twins. Harry picked up the doctors' roster. It was already a mess—a mass of red crossings-out and locums and gaps in the schedule, and that had been before Dr Vermont had so suddenly died.

'So much for leaving,' Harry said.

'What are you going to do?'

'I don't know,' Harry admitted. 'I've just about used up every last favour. I'll have to do something, though. I simply can't imagine this place without him. He and Marjorie were so good to me when Jill had her accident...' He hesitated, not sure if Marnie was interested in hearing his thoughts or if she was just being polite.

'Go on,' Marnie offered, but Harry looked over at the sleeping twins and shook his head. 'Not here.'

They moved to the small kitchenette where they could talk and still keep an eye on the children.

'Jill was on ICU for two weeks after the accident.' Harry paused for a moment, which he so rarely did—he simply didn't have the time or the reserves to examine the past, but the emotion of losing such a close friend and colleague forced a moment of reflection. 'Jill had massive head injuries.'

'How?'

'A car accident. The only saving grace was that she didn't have the twins with her at the time. I knew as soon as I saw her that things were never going to be the same again and so did Dr Vermont. Even if she had lived, her injuries were so severe that things would never have been the same,' Harry explained. 'Dr Vermont told me that the time Jill was on ICU was my time. I can't really explain it, but we both knew at some level how difficult things would be, whether she lived or died. Cathy, my sister, had the twins and brought them in now and then to see their mum.

'Dr Vermont took care of the department. Marjorie brought dinner in for me every night and clothes, and just did so many things for me that I didn't even notice. I was so focused on the time I had left with Jill. I think I did all my grieving in ICU. I have bad days of course, but, really, when she died it wasn't about Jill, or Jill and I any more, or me, it was about the twins and work and just surviving.' He looked at Marnie, suddenly aware that his words might be hurting her for reasons of her own. 'Was it the same for you?'

'No,' Marnie admitted. 'The whole time Declan was in ICU I was convincing myself that he'd live and making plans for taking him home. Right till the last day I thought that he'd make it.' Marnie shook her head—she just didn't want to go there.

As the day staff arrived and the news was broken there were tears on the floor and more tears in the staffroom. Marnie worked her way through the contact sheets, ringing the staff who were not on duty today, or not due in till later, to let them know what had happened.

It was a department in mourning but, of course, the patients continued to arrive.

'I've come to get the twins.' It was Harry's sister, Marnie could tell. Her face was strained and yet she gave Harry a hug when he came over.

'I'm sorry, Harry. I know he meant the world to you.'
'Thanks.'
'The thing is…'
Harry halted her.
'I know you can't keep doing this,' Harry said for her. 'If you can just help me out till the funeral.'

It was close to eleven by the time Marnie got home and she had to be back there at eight for her night shift.

Despite the warmth of the house, Marnie was shiv-

ering as she climbed into bed and recalled her last conversation with Dr Vermont.

This too will pass.

Yes, Marnie thought, her body tired but her mind
just too busy for sleeping.

When?

CHAPTER NINE

THERE WEREN'T JUST cracks appearing, there were gaping holes in the roster and a couple of nights Marnie was close to putting the department on bypass again. Harry's sister had taken the children for the rest of the week and he was covering the department as best he could but, of course, he couldn't work twenty-four hours a day. He told Admim that he would work till the funeral on Thursday but, after that, it was up to them to find a replacement.

Sheldon was looking boot-faced when he came on duty on the morning of the funeral to work alongside yet another locum and one he didn't particularly like.

'Harry's hardly going to miss the funeral,' Marnie pointed out. 'But cover's been arranged for the weekend. Helen Cummings is covering the night shifts and she's really good. I worked with her a lot at the Royal…'

'What about next week?' Sheldon said, but Marnie had no answer.

'Who's in charge this morning?' Lillian asked.

Marnie explained what had been arranged. 'Miriam's working till ten then going to the funeral. I'm going to have a couple of hours' sleep in the on-call room and then we're running a skeleton staff till two p.m. and the place will be on bypass.'

Marnie watched Lillian's lips disappear. Putting the department on bypass cost the hospital a lot in fines, but Marnie almost dared Lillian to question the decision on the day of Dr Vermont's funeral. It was going to be huge—several surgical lists had been rescheduled so that colleagues could pay their respects, a huge entourage would be leaving from the hospital, then there would be drinks and refreshments for those who wanted them after the official wake. Whoever had said no one was indispensable had never met Dr Vermont.

'We're all trying our best,' Marnie said. 'I called Dr Cooper but he can't start any sooner as he's working his notice till the last day. I think I might have to call Juan...'

'He's on his honeymoon.' Even the hard-nosed Lillian was reluctant to go that far, or perhaps she knew Juan too well. He was one of the rare few who had worked to get balance in his life and knew his priorities. Terminating his honeymoon wouldn't be an option. 'I doubt he's going to fly back from Argentina,' Lillian said, but Marnie just shrugged.

'Well, he is a consultant, perhaps he'd want to know that the place is collapsing.'

'Rather you than me,' Lillian said.

Marnie checked the local time in Argentina on the computer and, seeing it was early evening, decided to give it a try, but even the switchboard operator was reluctant to give her an outside line.

'Yes, it's a mobile I'm trying to call!' Marnie rolled her eyes at Miriam, who had just come on. 'Well, I don't know his landline number in Argentina, he could be anywhere. I just want to be put through to his mobile...' She was halted from continuing as the receiver was taken from her hand. Marnie turned to the delicious

sight of Harry in a black suit and tie and, though it was
expertly knotted, it was just a tiny bit off centre and his
collar needed arranging, but thankfully she managed to
resist, focusing instead on the gorgeous waft of cologne.

'Our mistake,' Harry said to the switchboard operator. He hung up the phone and then looked down at
Marnie. 'You'd really do it, wouldn't you?'

'Watch me!' Marnie said, trying to get at the phone,
but Harry blocked her.

'You cannot call a man on his honeymoon to fly
back to work.' Harry hadn't done a lot of smiling this
week and he was trying not to now as he looked down
in disbelief at Marnie. 'We're trying to prevent the next
consultant dropping dead from a heart attack, Marnie.'

'Well, I'd want to know.'

'Really?' Harry checked. 'Lying by the pool on your
honeymoon, next to the man of your dreams, you'd
really want a phone call telling you to get back here.'

'Ha,' Marnie said. 'I hate sunbathing and there'll be
no ring on this finger...' She held up that perfect finger in an almost inappropriate gesture. 'Anyway, Harry,
you've no right to be stopping me. Soon this place won't
be your problem any more.'

'Well, for this morning it still is and you are not
ringing Juan.'

'Fine,' Marnie said, and turned to Miriam. 'I'm going
to the doctors' on-call room to have a sleep. Wake me
when you want to start getting ready for the funeral.'
She looked back to Harry. 'Good luck today. Are you
speaking?'

'I am.' Harry grimaced. 'I'm just going to go and get
my car washed and then—'

'You should have washed it on your way home last
night.'

'I was tired.'

'Bet you wish you'd done it last night this morning!'

'No,' Harry lied. 'Actually, I'm going round to my office now to read through the speech and then go and sort out the car...'

'Keep it short.'

'Sorry?' She was telling him how to speak at a funeral!

'Short's better,' Marnie said.

'This from a woman who never stops talking? So you're an expert in funerals now, are you?'

'Actually, now you mention it...' She gave him a smile but then it turned to a more sympathetic one. 'I hope it goes as well as it can.'

'Thanks.'

'Harry.' She looked up at him, those blue eyes blazing, her lips worrying. 'I'm sorry, I just can't stop myself. It is a funeral you're going to after all...' Two very cold but terribly beautiful hands were at his neck, fixing his collar and tie.

'I can dress myself.'

'I know,' Marnie said, 'but you were right, Kelly.' She briefly glanced at Kelly, whose cheeks turned to ruby as she found out first hand that Marnie knew exactly what was being said about her. 'I think I do have a touch of OCD and I just cannot let you go without fixing your collar, Harry.' Oh, it was perfect now, collar down, knot in the centre. 'After all, you're representing the department!'

It wasn't intimate in the least, Harry told himself, and that was confirmed two minutes later when he saw her in the corridor, dusting down Eric's shoulders with a lint brush she just happened to keep in her office.

No, it wasn't intimate, but why could he still feel her fingers on his neck?

Why, when he saw from his office Marnie disappearing into the on-call room, did he sit there, wondering if she'd undress for bed?

Oh, help, Harry thought as she came out shoeless in stockinged feet with her hair down and returned a moment later with a pair of scrubs in her hand to change from that navy dress into pyjamas.

No, the little finger gesture hadn't been inappropriate—what was inappropriate was his thoughts on the morning of Dr Vermont's funeral.

He got up and closed the door, so as not to think of her.

It didn't work.

She'd drive you crazy, Harry told himself.

And as for bed, Harry attempted to alleviate the ache in his groin with the thought of Marnie moaning that she'd just changed the sheets, or maybe putting little towels down in case he dared to so much as spill a drop.

'Filthy business!' He could almost hear her saying it and, yes, that thought almost worked, except he remembered only too well their kiss and two minutes later Harry gave up focusing on the speech and headed out to get the car washed.

Anything for the distraction.

Marnie, his mind had decided, would be deliciously filthy.

'Marnie!'

Marnie peeled her eyes open as she heard Miriam's voice at the door. 'Marnie.'

'I'm up,' Marnie called, and on autopilot headed to

the sink and brushed her teeth. There was *nothing* worse than a two-hour sleep after a night shift.

Well, there was a whole lot worse, Marnie told herself as she washed her face, but the point she was making to herself was that getting up from a short sleep, when you really needed a long one, was one of the reasons she had always loathed nights.

Marnie stood shivering in scrubs and a cardigan in the kitchen, pouring herself a very strong coffee as Harry breezed in with a load of glasses that were on loan to the department. He did a double-take when he saw the usually very groomed Marnie a good inch shorter without her low heels and as pale as the milk she was pouring into her coffee.

'I know.' She rolled her eyes. 'It should be me they're burying today.'

She dealt with death and all the horrible stuff with a black, wry humour that would offend some, but never him. Somehow, on not quite Harry's worst day, but it was certainly there in the rankings, she made him smile.

It felt strange as everyone started to leave. The department was on bypass and quiet, but all morning it had been a hub of activity, a meeting centre. Abby's tears had already started as everyone filed out to get into the cars and Harry put his arm around Abby and then patted his pockets.

'Here,' Marnie said, handing him a box of tissues from the bench, and then they were gone.

The department was eerily quiet. The locum was calm and efficient with the few patients they had but there was an immense sadness that simply wouldn't abate. Every time Marnie looked at the clock or paused a moment she thought about that last conversation with Dr Vermont or wondered how Marjorie was faring.

Harry too.

For that morning, at least, the focus wasn't on rosters or filling in shifts, it was on the huge loss—the tremendous gap that a wonderful man had left.

Staff started to arrive early in the afternoon and the staffroom filled with hospital personnel—those who had been to the funeral and those who hadn't been able to get away for it.

'How was it?' Marnie asked Harry. He seemed beyond exhausted, but had that grim-faced look of just pushing through.

'Awful.' Harry wasn't stopping. 'I just came in to drop some supplies off. Marjorie asked me to take some of the food from the wake for everyone here. I told her it had all been catered but she wanted to contribute to it too. Can you help me get some stuff out of the car?'

'Sure.'

'Where are the twins today?' Marnie asked, as they walked out into the sunshine on what would normally feel a glorious day.

'At Cathy's till this evening.' There were mountains of food, tray after tray of sandwiches and boxes of drinks, and they ended up loading one of the gurneys and covering it with a sheet before pushing it through the department and round to the staffroom.

'So, this is your last day?' Marnie asked.

'It has to be,' Harry said, as they unloaded the food and set up. 'Cathy's had to take this week off work.' He didn't want to think about it now—for the most part, they had Friday and the weekend covered.

'You go home, Marnie.' Miriam, back from the funeral, her eyes red rimmed, took over unloading the boxes. 'You must be exhausted. I hope you're not driving.'

'No.' Marnie shook her head. 'I'm taking a taxi.'

'I'll drive you,' Harry said.

'Shouldn't you stay for a bit…?' Marnie started, and then stopped. After all, it was the story of Harry's life at the moment and the reason he had no option but to quit his job.

'They're talking about building an extension in his name,' Harry said. As they walked to his car, Marnie was shivering again. 'The Vermont Wing.'

'That would be nice.'

'Well, there won't be a Worthington Wing.'

'Just as well,' Marnie said as they climbed into his car. 'Try getting your lips around that after a night shift.'

Harry actually laughed. 'Beach Road?' he said, because he remembered everything she had ever told him.

'The dodgy end.' Marnie smiled.

'I can't believe he won't get to retire,' Harry said as they drove out of the hospital. His phone was bleeping away but he just ignored it. 'Though he'd have hated retirement—even Marjorie said as much—he loved that place.'

'You do too.'

Emotional blackmail wasn't going to work on Harry. He never took his eyes off the road. 'I love my kids. I need to put them first. Charlotte's becoming more precocious by the minute, Adam…' He liked it that she didn't push things, just waited as he voiced a potential problem that he hadn't discussed with anyone. 'I think he's got a speech delay.' His knuckles were white on the wheel. 'I've been thinking it for months and I haven't even had time to do a thing about it.'

'Looks like I'll be ringing Juan to come back from his honeymoon, then.'

'You really aren't romantic?'

'Not at all,' Marnie said. 'Men always have to complicate things.' She watched as Harry's tense mouth curved into a smile—his problem was the same, but with women, of course. 'They say they want an independent woman,' Marnie continued. 'They insist they do but then they get all misty-eyed and start to ask strange things like could I possibly iron a shirt? Or they think that just because you had sex last night it means you're going to be overtaken by this sudden urge to cook for them…'

Harry laughed, really laughed, for the first time since he'd taken the call about Dr Vermont. It wasn't the safest conversation to be having right now. He turned and glanced at her. There was a smile on her lips as she looked out of the window, a smile that told him she knew she was flirting. His phone bleeped again. Harry went to get it, but seeing cyclists up ahead knew better than to risk it, but he was worried that it might be work. 'Can you get it out my pocket?'

She most certainly could.

Harry was used to making strange requests such as that one, used to concentrating on stitching, or something similar, as someone found his phone and held it for him to speak into. He could feel her bony fingers against his chest as her hand slipped inside his jacket and Marnie could feel the heat from his skin through his shirt.

'Mind on the road, Harry,' Marnie said, and he smiled. The air was almost crackling between them. 'You've a text from Cathy.'

'Which means Charlotte,' Harry translated. 'At least it isn't work.'

'What you need,' Marnie said, 'is a wife.'

'I've got one,' Harry said, and in a gesture that certainly wasn't insolent—in fact, for Marnie it was the nicest thing he could have done—Harry held up his ring finger.

'I know,' Marnie said, because she did know. She had a son. It didn't go away because time had passed.

He pulled up at her house and opened up the message.

'So that's that, then,' Harry said as he read it.

'Sorry?'

'I wasn't going to say anything but I was hoping that I might be able to juggle things next week—the incubation period is just about up and there was this tiny window of possibility that the twins could go back to day care on Monday…' He gave a wry laugh as he read out the text. 'Charlotte has spots—don't worry, right now she's delighted.'

'Poor Atlas,' Marnie said as she watched the load he was carrying drop just a touch heavier on his shoulders. She looked at his profile and knew she'd miss him.

A lot.

'Do you need to get back?'

'I'll call her,' Harry said. 'And see how she is.' Except his phone battery was almost flat. 'Can I use yours?'

'Sure.' She went to go in her bag to get it but changed her mind. 'Use the landline.'

'Marnie…' Harry started, and then changed his mind. 'Sure, a coffee would be great.' It was a long drive to his sister's after all.

But Marnie was over playing games.

'Harry, you *know* we're going to sleep together. So we can make this all awkward and have a coffee that neither of us wants and then a quick fumble at the door…' She loved it when he smiled.

'Won't it complicate things?'

'There's nothing complicated about sex.' Marnie smiled. 'And we don't work together any more.'

'I think—'

But she halted him. 'You've done enough thinking for the day.'

She was possibly the perfect woman for Harry right now, he decided as he tasted her moist, full lips.

And there was nothing nicer than the warmth of his kiss when you were freezing, Marnie told herself as his arms slid around hers. And could there be anyone better than Harry to get your second wind with? Because suddenly Marnie wasn't remotely tired.

'Come on,' Marnie said. 'Let's get you to bed!'

But first he called Charlotte and congratulated her on her spots.

'I'll stop and get some more supplies before I come and get you,' Harry said. 'Yep. Don't worry, I won't get there till dinner.' Marnie was taking off her cardigan as Cathy must have come on the phone. 'She's worried I'm going to pick her up before she gets to eat your pizza.' He looked at Marnie as he talked on about how today had gone well. Well, as well as funeral could go. 'Thanks for this week,' Harry said. 'No, Cathy, I get it. I know you can't take another week off...' He hesitated. 'No.' Harry's response was firm. 'Mum and Dad are okay for the odd night, but it's not fair to ask for a week.'

They just stared for a very long moment and there was something lovely about no longer working together, something really nice about being two people who were quite comfortable keeping their sex lives separate from the rest of their lives.

They both knew the other's rules.

They'd both wanted the other on sight.

'Come here,' Harry said, and it took just two words. Marnie stepped into his space and Harry looked down, lingering a moment safe in the knowledge there was no need for holding back now.

'You drove me crazy this morning.'

'I know.'

'You always do.'

'I know.' Marnie smiled.

She felt his mouth on hers, felt her tongue slide in and, yes, it was nice not to think.

Marnie, though she would never admit it to herself let alone Harry, was taken slightly aback by her own reaction to his mouth. She'd missed it, had been thinking about their kiss far more than she perhaps ought, and now he was back, his mouth sinking into hers, its demand building. She opened her eyes and saw Harry's were closed and it was an incredible turn-on to see him simply indulge. So lovely to feel his hands stop fighting their need for contact and roam free, down her waist, then to her bottom, and despite his height they were an incredible fit, Marnie thought, so incredible that it would be terribly easy to forget about bed.

Harry lifted her top, slid it over her head and moaned as his hands felt the bare skin he had craved. His fingers unhooked her bra and his mouth was enough to make her sink to her knees with Harry joining her.

'Harry...' She pulled back and he opened his eyes, waited for the inevitable excuses and the reasons that this was a terrible idea, but he still didn't know Marnie.

'I need to have a shower,' Marnie said, and he laughed for the second time in a very short space of time and, no, he didn't mind the delay in proceedings, especially with what she said next. 'I'd like to be clean before we get dirty.'

Marnie headed into her bedroom and picked up the alarm. 'What time do you need to leave?' she asked.

'Six.'

'I'll set it for five, then.' She was almost clinical in her approach yet for Harry it was sexy. He liked independence; heaven knew, there were so many people dependent on him. He liked the rarity of Marnie and her utter ease, combined with the delicious trepidation that he felt as she headed for the shower.

He heard the taps turn on as he closed the curtains of her bay window and undressed. It was an adult reprieve that had been building and with someone who fascinated him more and more. Someone with whom he could be himself, or rather he could go back to the man he had once been.

Naked, he walked into the bathroom and pulled back the curtain, stood watching her washing her hair, and she opened her eyes and smiled.

'You didn't come empty-handed, I hope.'

'No.'

'Come in, then.'

He picked up the soap and put the little silver wrapper in the holder, and there was nothing to stop them now.

'I hate showers,' Marnie said, looking down as his large hands lathered the soap and then slid over her breasts. 'Or maybe I don't.' He was as slow and as deliciously thorough as she had thought he would be. Marnie watched as he soaped her breasts, her nipples stretching and puckering, and then she took the soap from him, lathered her hands and then dropped it.

It was Harry who paused, stared down as her hands stroked the length of him, over and over. He stood, staring as if in some delicious hypnotic trance that they'd be jolted out of any second. Marnie knew it too, she felt the swell and the lift of the balls she cupped in her hand and she was so turned on watching Harry that she wouldn't have cared if his hand hadn't halted her.

He was struggling to hold back, and he kissed her till he was back from the edge. The shiver that went through her had nothing to with exhaustion or cold as Harry lowered his head to her breast.

Her breasts had been on his mind for so long, that long glimpse of them nestled in her lacy bra had been dancing in his mind's eyes since the kiss in her office. The taste of her wet, warm flesh in his mouth was more than worth the wait.

Marnie watched his tongue taking its time, building her urgency, and before she even begged she watched as her nipple disappeared into to the soft vacuum of his mouth. She felt his hand slide up her thigh and she just about folded over, holding onto his head for support.

Maybe she did like showers after all, she thought as Harry tended to the other breast for a while, ensuring she was flushed and dizzy from his generous tastings before his mouth moved down.

'Harry...'

He ignored her, knelt down and parted her legs. He retrieved the soap and washed her intimately, teasing out her clitoris till it was as erect as he'd left her nipples and then burying his face in her sex as his fingers slid deep inside.

Marnie usually took for ever to come but not this afternoon. She was pressing Harry's head in, watching him feast, buckling her legs to him, then accidentally blasting them with cold water as she grabbed a tap for support as she gave in to his mouth.

Harry loved the icy blast to his shoulders as he felt her heat in his mouth; he loved hearing the very controlled Marnie losing it to his tongue then shivering in his arms.

'More hot I think…' Harry said.

It was steamy, it was lovely and Harry had but a few minutes' patience left in him. He stood and watched as she tore the wrapper and both looked down as she gave him a little stroke and a tease.

'Sometimes I look down and just smile,' Marnie said at the sight of her hands tenderly wrapping her present as she slid the condom down.

'We'll slip,' Marnie warned as he picked her up, and she slid down on his length and Harry did his best to hold her, hot and slippery in his hands; but there was just a little too much energy between them, the sex they wanted a touch too vigorous to assure safety. 'We're going to end up in Emergency,' Marnie warned as he tried to get back to her breasts and she wrapped her legs tighter around him.

'They might have to send the flying squad out to us,' Harry said, giving up on the pleasure of her wet breast. She put her arms around his neck and still they kissed, but it was terribly difficult in her tiny shower and Harry wanted to see more of her.

He turned the taps off and carried her to the bed, letting her back till her shoulders rested and Marnie looked up to the stunning sight of him, dripping wet and devouring her with his eyes.

Her ankles were wrapped around his hips and he had one hand under her buttocks, the other stroking her as he thrust into her, but she pushed his hand away and gave full invitation.

She'd thought Harry sexy but she knew now just how sexy he was. Felt the grip of his hands on her hips and the delicious sight of him for once concentrating on himself. It was bliss to be moved by him, to be taken. The slap of wet skin and the feel of Harry unleashed deep inside, so potent even the soles of Marnie's feet seemed to contract as she started to writhe beneath him, not that Harry let her go anywhere.

He held her hips so tight as he shot into her that Marnie fought to arch, the suppression forcing the channels of energy back to where Harry delivered his final thrusts deep inside her. It tipped Marnie into the deepest orgasm of her life—her thighs shaking, her bottom lifting, grateful for the hands that held her firm as she rode the deep waves that coursed through her.

And Harry watched her collapse.

He could hardly breathe, he could see the flush on her cheeks and breasts and the tension in her throat as she spasmed around him. He watched and felt as slowly it all dissipated, yet the sight was almost enough for him to go again.

Yet almost better than the sex for Harry was afterwards. He kept waiting for the comedown, and so did Marnie, but right now it was just a matter of sleeping.

For the first time in what felt like for ever the world was a worry-free zone.

CHAPTER TEN

'PRESS SNOOZE,' MARNIE said.

'It's on your side.'

It was very hard, trying to reach the alarm with Harry spooned into her and his strong arm holding her tight.

Marnie pressed snooze and felt his erection nudging, pulled a little packet from the drawer and, really, she'd have loved not to bother. And Harry would have loved not to bother either.

They were too sensible for that.

It did break the moment, though, a moment that neither usually minded breaking, but Harry soon got back behind her. 'Where were we?' he asked, nuzzling the back of her neck. The alarm going off the second time didn't actually ruin things as she reached over and turned it off. It felt natural for Harry to pull her back to his warm body and slide himself in.

Marnie loved half waking to Harry. She loved this slow, lazy sex where she barely had to move, and she loved his breath in her ear.

'I remember you now,' Harry said. 'I offered to buy you a drink.'

'No,' Marnie corrected, as he rocked deep inside her. 'The drinks were free that night.'

'I offered to get you a drink…'

'No,' Marnie corrected again, but she couldn't really think straight. She was trying to turn her head to meet his mouth, trying to stop her own orgasm because she didn't want it over just yet, or maybe she did because conversation was forgotten now as both surrendered to the bliss and then lay there for a few moments afterwards. Harry stroked her stomach; Marnie felt him soften and gradually slip away.

She didn't want him to leave.

Harry didn't particularly want to go home either. On a wretched, black day he'd glimpsed peace and it would be so incredibly easy to just drop all balls completely and close his eyes and sleep.

But he never would.

'I'd better go soon.'

She turned to him and decided that, yes, he'd better because she was so comfortable, so warm, so *enjoying* being with him; it would be too easy to kiss him, or for them to both close their eyes and convince themselves they could wake up if they had just five minutes' more sleep.

'Go on.' She disentangled herself and for Harry it was incredibly hard to haul himself out of bed.

'When the twins are better...'

'Harry...' She shook her head, didn't really want to spell out to him that a single father of two wasn't quite the date she had in mind.

He picked up his shirt and held it up. 'You couldn't give this a quick iron, could you?'

'Don't even joke.'

As he did up his shirt, Harry caught sight of a blonde Marnie holding her son and, yes, he hadn't been lying, he did remember her now.

'I asked why you were leaving,' Harry said. 'You didn't answer.'

'Yes, well, you wouldn't have liked it if I had,' Marnie said. 'I'd just found out I was pregnant.'

'What went wrong?' He wondered if he'd asked too much. There were so many no-go areas with Marnie—it would seem from her previous response that dinner and a bottle of wine was a no-no, yet, Harry realised as she started to answer him, she was prepared now to talk a little about her son.

'Premature,' Marnie said. 'Poor little thing didn't stand a chance—I had a placenta the size of an AA battery...' It was a dark joke and Harry didn't smile; he just picked up the photo and looked at them both as Marnie spoke on. 'So not only was he premature, he was also small for dates. Then he got an HAI and was just too small to fight it.'

No wonder she was obsessive about hand-washing and curtains being changed, Harry thought—a hospital-acquired infection explained a lot of things but it was as if she'd read his thoughts.

'I was always a clean-freak.' Marnie smiled. 'Even before Declan got so ill but, yes, I go a bit overboard at work.'

'I don't blame you.'

'You'd better go,' Marnie said. It felt strange to watch him holding her picture. It felt strange to be discussing that time with anyone other than Siobhan, who, even on the other side of the world, still nursed her through the yearly hell of birthdays and anniversaries and all the things you really needed a cuddle for, but a computer screen or telephone call had to suffice.

Harry didn't want to go, not just because he wanted to climb back into bed and forget the world for a moment. It was more that there was so much to Marnie that he'd like to know, so much about today he was having trouble letting go of.

So many things that he didn't want to end, and so he tried again.

'Do you want to go out at the weekend?'

'I'd imagine you'd have trouble getting a babysitter for twins with chickenpox.'

'I guess...' He felt strange walking off, as if he'd been using her, when for Harry it had been anything but. 'Have you had chickenpox?'

'I have.'

'Maybe you could come over. I could cook.'

'Harry, don't spoil it.' She was incredibly direct.

She made no excuses, Harry noticed as he dressed, and he should be glad of it. Glad for a woman who knew what she wanted—and a single dad to twins wasn't high on her list.

She was just moving to the top of his.

Marnie was lying in bed, watching him as he did up his tie but then, as he came over and sat down to kiss her goodbye, she suddenly found a solution.

This too will pass.

She could almost hear Dr Vermont say the words.

'Thank God we don't work together...' Harry gave a rueful smile as she reached for his tie and, as Marnie so loved to do, straightened it.

'About that,' Marnie said.

'About what?'

'Do you have a bath?'

'Yes.'

'How about I move in for a week?'

Harry grinned. 'This from a woman who doesn't even want to come out with me for dinner.'

'I'm not talking about dating or romance,' Marnie said. 'I'm talking about me moving in and, between us, taking care of the children. Harry, you're in the eye of the storm at the moment but in a week's time you'll have your lady back to help with the children, Juan will be working... If by then you still want to take yourself off and become hand surgeon of the year...' She made a little joke and then stopped because actually she was completely serious. 'My moving in for a week would give you a pause.'

'Why would you do that?'

'Because, I don't want the department that I've just started running to fall apart.'

'I can't drag you from your home.'

'It's hardly a home,' Marnie said. 'I've only been here five minutes!'

She simply didn't get attached to anything, Harry realised, but it would be so very easy to get attached to her, and he wasn't just thinking about himself when he spoke.

'It would be too confusing for the children,' he said, because, for all his faults, he had managed to keeps his flings well away from them, and Marnie in his bed for a week... He shook his head but then realised that for Marnie this *was* strictly business.

She really could separate the two.

'I'm not going to be sleeping with you, Harry, especially if there's a chance we are going to continue working together. There'll be no confusion.' Marnie smiled. 'I only want you professionally, Harry. It will be a working arrangement.'

'I can't ask you to take time off work to look after my kids.'

'Who said anything about that? I have the weekend

off already, a day off in lieu of nights on Monday, and
I'll take a management day on Tuesday and sort out
those bloody rosters once and for all from home.'

His mind was turning faster. It was maybe, possibly doable.

'I could do a couple of nights on the days you're
working. If I can sit down with Helen and work out
some shifts...'

'We can work it,' Marnie said. 'It's just one week. I
need a doctor for my department, Harry. I have no intention of failing.'

He looked at Marnie, sitting on the bed, the tiniest
yet strongest woman he had ever met, and the most determined too. 'I doubt you could.'

CHAPTER ELEVEN

'I FEEL LIKE Mary Poppins,' Marnie said as Harry opened his front door.

'Oh, you're no Mary Poppins.' Harry grinned, taking her case. He was looking more rumpled than usual and that clean-shaven look of yesterday was fading. 'Come in. Charlotte's just starting to realise that chickenpox isn't so much fun after all.'

No, Marnie was no Mary Poppins. Mary was a good girl who didn't notice things like Harry's bum as she followed him through to the lounge, but, then, she'd never seen Harry in just a T-shirt and jeans and barefoot too. Oh, she'd seen him in a suit, in scrubs and stark naked, but there was something very attractive about him in a T-shirt because it showed off his very flat stomach and in jeans his legs just looked longer.

No, she was no Mary Poppins, but Marnie was still a good girl because she didn't give that bottom a pinch as they walked and she kept her thoughts well to herself too—butter wouldn't have melted in her mouth as she gave his children a smile.

'This is Marnie,' Harry introduced her. 'You both met her at the hospital.'

Adam looked up and smiled and said hello, but Charlotte's eyes narrowed. 'A nurse isn't a nanny.'

'I'm not a nanny,' Marnie said. 'I'm here to help look after you so that Daddy can work.'

'Have you looked after children before?'

'Charlotte,' Harry warned.

'It's fine,' Marnie said. 'I don't mind being inter-viewed—I'd want to know who was looking after me too.' She turned to Charlotte. 'I've looked after plenty of children and I have lots of nieces and nephews and many younger brothers, so I've have a bit more of a head start than most.'

Harry showed her around—it was a lovely old home, though the stairs creaked terribly as Harry lifted her case upstairs.

'It's a beautiful home.'

'It's needs a demolition ball,' Harry said. 'It looks nice but everything needs fixing, apart from this...'

He opened a door and Marnie almost whimpered at the sight of a beautiful bathroom—it was completely white except for a few dots of dark tiles on the floor. 'It's the one thing that has been renovated,' Harry said. 'I think they gave up after that. I can't wait to see the back of it.'

Marnie was surprised. Surely this home would be filled with memories and the last thing he would want was to let it go, but he must have read her confusion.

'Oh, no...' Harry shook his head. 'We'd just sold our house and were looking for somewhere when Jill died... It was hell—the buyers had sold too and there was no getting out of it. I didn't want the upheaval for the children.'

'Poor things.' It just poured out of her mouth. 'I hated moving, more than anything, I hated leaving Ireland and then when we had to leave Perth...' Marnie stopped. She didn't really like talking about herself but she was just trying to say that she understood how hard it must have been for the children to move so close to losing their mum.

'It wasn't exactly great timing,' Harry said when Marnie went quiet, 'but there was no real choice, so I rented this. Your friend Dave put me onto it.'

'Ah, Dave!' Marnie gave a bitter smile.

'It was supposed to be for six months…' He turned round and there was Charlotte, standing at the top of the stairs watching them.

'I'm itchy,' she said.

'I'll just show Marnie her room and then I'll come and put some cream on.'

They walked down the hall and he opened a door and put Marnie's case inside. 'I hope this is okay.'

'It's lovely.' It was, a large room with an iron bed dressed in white linen and lovely wooden furnishings that mismatched perfectly.

Charlotte, who had followed them, stood in the doorway and watched as Harry showed Marnie how the dodgy windows worked. 'Do you want to come in and help me put some things away?' Marnie offered.

'We're not allowed in the nanny's room,' Charlotte said, and huffed off.

'Fair enough,' Marnie said.

'She's normally much more friendly.'

'She's normally not covered in spots,' Marnie pointed out, as Harry, a touch awkward now, headed for the door. 'Do you want to go through our diaries?' Marnie suggested. 'Get it out of the way?'

'Sure.'

'I'll just unpack and I'll be down.'

Marnie unpacked her case—it only took a moment. She put her clothes in the wardrobe and hung her dressing gown up on the door and sorted out her toiletries. She put Declan's photo in the drawer of the bedside table. She didn't want questions if the children came peeking, but she couldn't bear to leave him at home, then she headed downstairs.

It was a working arrangement.

They sat at a large table and drank tea as they tried to sort out the upcoming week. 'I phoned Helen and I've got the shifts she can do, as well as Lazlo, he's on now and I'm going in tomorrow.'

'Who's Lazlo?'

'He used to work there and said that he can come in for a couple of shifts...'

Marnie looked at the schedule and saw Harry pencilled in for a shift on Friday night.

'I'm out that night,' Marnie said, and didn't elaborate, but Harry's jaw did tighten just a fraction as he recalled that she was going to the ballet.

With Matthew.

'Not a problem.' Harry cleared his throat before continuing. 'Okay, if I can get Helen to cover that night I can, if it's okay with you, be on call for the rest of the weekend and then Juan's back.'

It *was* a working arrangement.

She made that very clear.

When Harry opened a bottle of wine once the kids had gone to bed, Marnie politely declined.

'I'm going to have that bath.'

'Sure.'

She was a strange person, Harry thought—Marnie didn't even come down and say goodnight. But, ages later, when he headed for bed himself, he could hear her chatting away in her room and it took a moment for it to click that she was on the computer.

'You're living with him?' Siobhan checked, and Marnie was very glad for her headphones. 'You've slept with him and you've moved in but there's nothing going on?'

'You're making this more complicated than it is,' Marnie said.

'What does Matthew have to say about it?'

'I don't discuss things like that with Matthew,' Marnie said, but she did worry for a moment. 'Matthew and I...' She looked at Siobhan, who'd been married for nine years now and just loved hearing about friends with benefits and her best friend's rather glamorous life. 'I don't know,' Marnie admitted.

'What would Harry have to say about Matthew?'

'Nothing!' Marnie said. 'Because he's not going to find out.'

Except Harry had been there when Matthew had invited her to the ballet.

Marnie's conscience was pricking as she turned off the computer and tried to get to sleep.

She and Harry had been a one-off, an indulgence, safe in the knowledge they wouldn't be working together again.

See what happens when you take your eye off the ball, Marnie scolded herself.

It certainly wouldn't be happening again.

No, there was no hint of anything. The next morning she was up and dressed and even had lipstick on as Harry held up the kettle and asked if she wanted tea.

'Leave the tea bag in this time,' Marnie said.

'You're sure you don't mind doing this?' Harry checked. 'Charlotte's been up half the night crying. It's hardly a great day off for you.'

'Harry, I'm just relieved to know that the place is being looked after. It's been nothing but a headache trying to get the department covered.' She turned as Adam came down. 'Good morning.'

'Morning, Marnie.'

She was *lovely* to Adam. She chatted away and found out that he'd like cornflakes and juice and yet, Harry couldn't put his finger on it, she still held back. Then Charlotte appeared.

'Do you want babies?' Charlotte asked as Marnie sorted out her breakfast.

'Charlotte,' Harry scolded.

'It's fine.' Marnie smiled. 'No, Charlotte, I don't want babies.'

'Why?'

'Because...' Marnie filled a bowl with cornflakes as she spoke '...I like my work, I like my holidays, I like lots of things. And,' Marnie added, 'as I told you, I had lots of younger brothers. I've changed more nappies than most!'

'Don't scratch,' Harry warned, as Charlotte started to.

'I keep forgetting.'

'I'll paint your nails red later,' Marnie said. 'That will remind you.'

After Harry had gone, she did paint Charlotte's nails red and then she went about opening the windows and stripping the beds between putting on anti-itch cream at various times throughout the day.

'Do you like our house?' Charlotte asked as she showed her the cupboard at the top of the stairs where the fresh sheets were kept.

'I think it's lovely,' Marnie said, as she pulled out some sheets. 'Right! Which ones are yours, Adam?'

'The blue ones, silly,' said Charlotte. 'Mine are pink.'

* * *

Harry could not have done it without her.

The children could not have been better looked after and a wary Charlotte had quickly warmed to Marnie's chatter and rather offbeat humour. Despite refusing to iron a thing for Harry, Marnie hauled out the ironing board on the Tuesday evening and made a major dint in the piles of children's bedding and clothing.

'Do you ever stop?' Charlotte asked. She was helping Marnie to fold things as a distraction from scratching.

'Not till the work's done,' Marnie said.

Only Harry noticed that Charlotte's smile wavered.

CHAPTER TWELVE

'YOU'VE DONE WELL during an extremely difficult time.'

She was sitting in a management meeting. Lillian had blinked a bit at the budget report, and there had been a couple of explosions. The maintenance hours had trebled and there had been fines for the department for twice being on bypass. That had been nothing to do with lack of beds or waiting times, though—in fact, waiting times were down as Marnie was very clued up about the wards hiding beds and had threatened a few times to go up and make a bed herself unless the patient was accepted soon.

Patient complaints were down too.

Marnie put out fires as they happened rather than letting them simmer and, overall, she was pretty pleased as she made her way back down to the department.

No one knew she was staying at Harry's. Certainly no one could know that the reason she hadn't arrived until ten past nine this Thursday was because of the patient Harry had been stuck with. There had been a couple of raised brows as she'd rushed in because she was so rarely late.

But, apart from that, things had ticked along.

Marnie was enjoying her time with the twins—she liked children. She had been adored by her brothers as they'd grown up and was now a favourite aunty. Yes, she liked children, she just didn't want any of her own.

She'd had her baby and wasn't going to put herself through it ever again—she admired those that did.

Making her way back from the meeting, Marnie walked into the pre-natal ward and couldn't help peeking in.

'Hello!' She knocked on the open door and smiled as Emily looked up from the book she was writing in.

'Marnie!'

'Am I disturbing you?'

'Not at all.' Emily smiled. 'I'm on bed rest till the baby is born. I've never been more up to date with my homework.'

Marnie looked at the huge pile of books by her bed. 'You've got no excuse not to get a good grade,' Marnie said. 'How have your parents been?'

'They've been marvellous!' Emily said. 'I can't believe how good they've been, even though I do I think Dad's disappointed.'

'Maybe he's just worried,' Marnie offered.

'I guess,' Emily said, 'but we've spoken about what we're going to do and they're looking at doing up the granny flat so that Reece and I can live in that.'

'Wow.' Marnie smiled.

'Reece has got another job while I'm on bed rest…'

'You're going to get there,' Marnie said. 'It sounds like you're both using this time to put your heads down and get a future happening.'

'We will.' Emily nodded. 'I wanted to nurse before all this happened but now I'm thinking of teaching.'

'You'll get school holidays off!' Marnie smiled. 'And that's something to think about because, by the time you're qualified, you'll almost have a school-aged child.'

She looked at a very mature seventeen-year-old. 'What a great teacher you'd be,' Marnie said, 'having already earned your qualifications in the school of life.'

'Thanks, Marnie.'

'I shall come and see you again, if you like.'

'I'd love it.'

That night she told Harry about visiting Emily as they ate dinner before Harry went to work.

Charlotte and Adam had already eaten and were making a lot of noise upstairs as cabin fever started to seriously hit.

'I stopped in on Emily today. She's doing really well.' Marnie smiled. 'She's got her head down studying, hoping to be a teacher, and Reece is working an extra job.'

'They still have to be teenagers, though,' Harry said, mashing butter into his potato.

'She won't have time for being a teenager once the baby comes along. It's good that she's getting ahead.' Marnie stopped. Even she could hear that she sounded like her own mother and she tried to soften it. 'It's going to be hard for her but Emily will get there.'

'Did you work right through your pregnancy?'

'I went on bed rest when it was clear my placenta was failing,' Marnie said. 'But I'd have been straight back to my studies even if Declan…' She really didn't like talking about it. There was an uncomfortable silence and after a moment Harry filled it.

'What were your friends like?' Harry asked.

'Siobhan was great,' Marnie said. 'She's my best friend in Ireland, but can you believe she came all this way for the funeral? She'd saved up enough to go travelling for a year and she spent half of it getting here to help console me.'

'What about the girls you trained with?'

'Scathing.' Marnie pulled a face. 'Well, they weren't really friends, we'd all started just a few months back, and I think they thought I was mad to be going through with it.'

'And after you lost him?'

'It was awkward,' Marnie admitted. 'They were busy being teenagers and I guess I wasn't my sunniest. I took my nursing very seriously…'

Oh, he could just imagine that she had!

'That's why I transferred to the Royal. I just didn't want to be around anyone who knew what had happened so I gave myself a fresh start. Of course, I was always an old head on young shoulders even before…' She looked up at him. 'I did know what was involved having a baby—I was nearly eleven when mum had Ronan. I got up to him at night. It might have been an accident but I did know what I was taking on.'

Harry took the plates to the sink. He could see her sitting there, staring, and he thought about a teenage Marnie, let loose for the first time. Those first few months of freedom and, oh, what a price…

'Marnie. Why don't—?'

'I'm going to get the children ready for bed.' She just halted him. Marnie didn't want pensive conversations that changed nothing. 'You're off tomorrow?' Marnie checked their plans before she headed off.

'Yep, but I'm on all weekend.' He felt as guilty as hell, not that Marnie seemed to mind.

'That's fine. What time do you have to be in Saturday morning?'

'Eight.'

'I'll make sure I'm back early, then.'

'Early?'

'Saturday morning,' Marnie said. 'I told you I'm out Friday.'

'Of course...' Harry shook his head. 'I forgot.'

He hadn't forgotten, not for a moment, he'd just kind of hoped things might have changed.

But, then, why would they?

Marnie wasn't giving her heart away to anyone.

CHAPTER THIRTEEN

'I've booked The Langham.'

Marnie was trying to get Charlotte to brush her teeth when Matthew called.

Marnie loved The Langham—it was a beautiful hotel on the river and possibly her favourite place on earth, but not even the prospect of The Langham could soothe a rather awkward conversation.

'Who's that?' Matthew asked, as a very demanding Charlotte called out for Marnie.

'I'm just watching a friend's children for a couple of days.' She didn't give him a moment to question it. 'I'll try to get there for six.'

'Who were you speaking to?' Charlotte asked, when Marnie hung up.

'A friend,' Marnie said. 'And you should be paying more attention to your teeth than my phone calls—you didn't do the back ones.'

'I hate brushing my teeth.'

'I'd noticed!' Marnie said. 'You'll end up like Adam.' Marnie smiled at Charlotte's brother. 'All your teeth will fall out. Show me…' she said, and Adam took his finger and wobbled a tooth that was barely hanging. Marnie felt a curl in her stomach as he pushed it too far.

'Stop now!' Marnie said, but Adam just laughed and wiggled it harder.

They were fun but exhausting and, as Marnie cleaned up the bathroom, she told herself there'd be fluffy towels and champagne waiting tomorrow.

It just didn't cheer her as much as it usually would.

Marnie was in bed early, knowing the chances of a full night's sleep were remote, and that was confirmed at two a.m.

'Daddy!' Marnie heard Charlotte's first cry and got up and headed to go to her, then turned and put a dressing gown on over her pyjamas.

'It's Marnie, Charlotte,' Marnie said, as she opened the door. 'Daddy's at work, remember—I'm looking after you tonight.'

'I itch.'

'I know,' Marnie said. 'It's that horrible chickenpox but they'll be gone soon. Shall I put on some lotion?'

Charlotte nodded.

'Would you like a drink?'

Charlotte nodded at that suggestion too.

'Why don't you go off to the loo,' Marnie said, 'and I'll be back with a drink and some nice cold cream?'

Marnie was very used to patients waking at two a.m. and more often than not it was the need to go to the toilet that had woken them. So she turned on the lights for Charlotte and then headed down the stairs, made her a drink and found the cream.

Charlotte was back in bed by the time Marnie got back up there and, despite the hour, Charlotte was her usual talkative self as Marnie dabbed on the cream.

'What's a code blue?'

'Why do you ask that?'

'Code red is for a fire and all the doors close,' Charlotte said, and Marnie's hand paused as she realised that the children must hear the overhead intercom alerts in the crèche. Well, of course they would, Marnie reasoned. If there was a fire or the crèche needed to be evacuated, then they needed to hear the alerts too, but it didn't sit right with Marnie that the twins heard them.

'So,' Charlotte pushed. 'What's a code blue?'

'It's when certain doctors are needed.'

'Like the trauma team?'

'Yes,' Marnie said. 'Right, you're done.' As Charlotte lay down Marnie tucked the sheet in around her and went to turn out the light. ''Night, Charlotte. You just call if you need anything.'

'Can you read me a story?'

'I'll tell you a story,' Marnie said, because the light was already off and Charlotte didn't need any more stimulation. Marnie sat on the edge of the bed and told her the same stories she had told Ronan when he had been little. About the fairies that lived at the bottom of the garden and all the good work that they did.

'In your garden?' Charlotte asked.

'In my garden back home in Ireland.'

'But what happens when you move?' Charlotte asked, and Marnie had been about to say they stayed to help the next lot of children who lived there but she could hear the anxiety in Charlotte's voice. She remembered that they'd already moved at a very difficult time and would perhaps soon be moving again.

'The fairies move with you,' Marnie explained, and in the darkness she could see Charlotte's eyes shining, waiting for her to go on. 'They fly along with the removal truck.'

'So the fairies from our old house are here?'

'Of course they are,' Marnie said. 'We'll take a little treat down for them at the weekend.'

Charlotte seemed to like that idea and it was she who said goodnight this time, but as Marnie went to go Charlotte halted her.

'Did your fairies move with you?'

'Of course,' Marnie said, but if she'd been making things up before, now she really was lying. All the lovely imaginings of her childhood were still there in Ireland, all the games and the fun and the innocence were still there in her old home and garden.

'Maybe not all of them, though.' Charlotte yawned. 'Fairies are very small and Australia is a long way to fly.'

She really did need to get out more, Marnie told herself as she climbed into bed, because all this talk of fairies and flying and her fairies being left behind had Marnie suddenly on the edge of crying.

It had been an emotional time, she told herself. The department was struggling not just with the doctor shortage but with the aching gap Dr Vermont himself had left behind.

But it wasn't just that.

She'd never expected she might get attached to Charlotte and Adam—Marnie's heart lived on ice—yet getting up to them at night, hearing their chatter, the things they said that made her laugh… Marnie could almost hear the drip of her heart thawing and it wasn't just that she didn't want it to, or that it terrified her, there was also an appalling sense of guilt because she was a mother of one and in a few days' time it would be Declan's birthday.

Not here!

Marnie lay in bed and refused to give in to tears—

she was here to look after children. What if Charlotte called or Adam woke up?

She needed tomorrow, Marnie told herself as she lay there, trying to picture the ballet while frantically trying not to picture afterwards.

She wanted a night at The Langham with Harry.

Or just a night with Harry would do.

'Marnie!' She was almost asleep when she heard her name called.

'I'm coming,' Marnie said once she had ungritted her teeth, grateful for the three a.m. reminder of why she didn't want a single father!

She needed a night away to get back to herself and normality, instead of crying over fairies and made-up stories.

Harry let himself in the following morning a little earlier than usual. The place had been quiet and he'd slept most of the night in the on-call room.

He was greeted by the sight of Marnie's small case and a slightly flustered Marnie who, as usual, was fully dressed and had her hair tied back and make-up on.

'I was just taking that out to my car.'

She'd hoped to do so before Harry got home or the children were up. She'd hoped to completely avoid any discussion about tonight.

She was looking after his children, Marnie told herself as she took out the small case. Certainly she was entitled to a night off.

Harry was trying to tell himself the same. 'How were the twins?' he asked, as she came back in.

'I never heard a peep from Adam, and Charlotte just got up a couple times because she was itchy.' She hesitated a moment, it was none of her business after all.

'She was asking what a code blue was and things. Did you know they hear all the intercoms?'

'I know,' Harry said. 'They have to be on.'

'Even so...'

'Marnie, I'd love them to be somewhere local but I struggle to get across the corridor to pick them up as it is.'

'Of course.' She changed the subject. The child-care arrangements really had nothing to do with her after all. She just loathed the hospital being so much a part of their young worlds.

Except it wasn't her place to loathe it.

'You'll be tired, watching them all day,' Marnie said.

'I got a few hours' sleep last night,' Harry said. 'Anyway, I'm not working tonight.'

'No.'

'About tonight...' Harry turned to fill the kettle, trying to work out what to say. He'd hoped for a busy night so he wouldn't have had time to dwell on it. What had happened to the wild Harry of old, or even the not-so-wild Harry of late who would have loved a woman who didn't want to get serious...?

He loved this woman.

No.

He tore his head from that thought, told himself that he was just a bit infatuated, that was all. Intrigued perhaps. Or maybe it was just his ego because the one woman who didn't want him...

The one woman.

'I think the kettle's full,' Marnie said, as water gushed into the sink.

'Daddy!' Charlotte was delighted to see him. 'Morning, Marnie.'

'Morning, Charlotte.'

'Can we take the treat to the fairies today.'

'I'm off to work,' Marnie said.

'When you get home, then?'

'I'm away tonight,' Marnie said, but again didn't elaborate. 'I'd better get going.'

It wasn't even eight o'clock.

'See you, Marnie...' Charlotte was hanging by the door as Marnie put her jacket on, and Marnie gave Charlotte a lovely smile and a wave as she headed out the door, but it was clear to Harry that Charlotte wanted a kiss.

Yes, they all wanted more from Marnie.

She'd be gone on Monday, he told himself.

It would be a relief, because it was killing him to have her here yet not.

In bed at night.

But not his.

CHAPTER FOURTEEN

THE DAY WENT far faster for Marnie than it did for Harry.

While he was trying not to pace at home and trying not give any leeway to the mounting disquiet that churned every time he thought of her out on her date tonight, Marnie never got a moment to think till she was flying through the door to her home just before five.

She'd left work early for once and, incredibly organised, her overnight bag was already packed. Even as she undressed, Marnie had flicked on her heated rollers and turned on the taps.

Okay, she conceded as she pulled on a shower cap and hopped under the water, showers were good for some things—at least she didn't have to wait for a bath to fill.

And showers were good for other things too, Marnie thought dreamily, recalling Harry, his hands soaping her body.

Marnie didn't really do feelings and as for loyalty, she wasn't deep enough into anyone to demand such a thing—but her moral compass was spinning in circles as, turned on for Harry, she turned off the taps and did her best to get ready...

For Matthew.

Her hair she piled into rollers.

Her make-up she had down pat and she was soon painted and sitting on the edge of the bed, pulling on gorgeous underwear and stockings and then arranging her cleavage into a very lacy bra. She took out her dress and laid it out on the bed—it was a gorgeous deep navy in the softest velvet and had cost a small fortune.

Yes, all the things she could afford because she didn't have children, and it wasn't just the financial benefits Marnie was taking into account as she quickly dressed—there was time to stop and get her nails done, time to linger in the make-up department, splurge on the ballet and a night at The Langham without having to worry about babysitters.

She wanted this life, Marnie insisted to herself. But her hands were shaking and she tipped on far too much perfume.

She'd been desperate to go when she'd heard the ballet was on—especially as it was Declan's birthday next week. She'd known she'd want a night staring in the dark and just seeing beauty, and then sex for sex's sake at a beautiful five-star hotel with her friend with benefits. Matthew didn't even know about Declan—he'd made a brief comment when he'd seen the silvery lines on her stomach and she'd mumbled something about being a fat teenager.

Marnie pulled out her rollers and sorted her hair, smiled at her reflection because she looked like some high-class tart standing fully made up in her underwear.

She'd be pushing it to get to the hotel, so she dressed quickly, doing up the zipper and then putting on her shoes before transferring all she'd need from her handbag into her evening bag.

'Tickets might help,' she told herself, and unzipped the flap in her bag, and then Marnie stilled.

'Oh, no!'

She'd put them in her computer bag. Marnie remembered now but it didn't stop her from tipping out her handbag in the futile hope that they'd suddenly appear—that she wouldn't have to stop by at Harry's to get them.

It's tickets! Marnie told herself.

She was simply making a big deal of it.

If she rang and warned Harry that she was on her way, then she might not even have to see him; she could just let herself in, fly up the stairs and fly out.

It really was no big deal, Marnie told herself as she dialled Harry's number.

'Harry!' Marnie cringed at her own voice, it came out too jolly and bright. 'I just need to stop by and grab something…'

'Something?' The last thing he needed was to see her on her way out. What if that bloody Matthew was driving her? No, he didn't like the idea of Matthew sitting in the car outside, but how could he put it delicately? 'I think it might be a bit confusing for the children.'

'Confusing?' Marnie checked—was this man serious? 'Did your previous nannies not go out?'

'Of course they did. I meant—'

'So the children won't be confused,' Marnie said, snapping off the phone.

It was the adults who were confused.

Harry was making dinner when he heard her key in the door and her breezy call, and he just called out hi and carried on chopping.

'Marnie…' Adam shouted. 'Look.'

Adam, who never asked for attention, was asking for it now. She could see him standing in the living room, holding his lips open like a horse.

'Adam's tooth came out,' Charlotte informed Marnie. 'He was eating popcorn.'

Marnie walked down the hallway and looked at Adam's gap and said all the right things as Harry stood in the open kitchen, chopping away. He felt like the most boring person in the world. He should be wearing a cardigan and slippers, Harry thought to himself. He was doing his best not to look up as Charlotte chatted.

'So the fairies will come tonight...' She stopped talking long enough to take in Marnie in her very lovely velvet dress and very, very high-heeled shoes. 'Marnie! You look...' Charlotte turned round to her dad. 'Doesn't she look beautiful, Daddy?'

Harry had no choice but to look.

In a very dark navy—or was it black?—velvet dress, she had stockings on and high heels and her hair was curly and worn down, her cleavage was gleaming white and her lips were painted red. Harry took a moment to find his voice.

'Very nice.'

'Where are you going?' Adam asked.

'Just out.'

'Where?' Adam persisted.

'Adam!' Harry warned, and then he let Marnie know he knew *exactly* what was going on. 'Marnie's going to the ballet, aren't you, Marnie?'

'I want to go to the ballet,' Charlotte said. 'I'm going to start ballet, aren't I? Soon, Daddy—you said, didn't you?'

He could barely get them home for dinner on time, Harry thought—try adding in dance lessons too. Only it wasn't Charlotte's excitement and chatter that had him chopping and chopping, it wasn't that Marnie was going out and he was at home, and it wasn't her free-dom. It was none of those things.

It was jealousy.

It was possessiveness that was filling his throat from the stomach up. A black jealousy that was as sickly and sweet and as potent as the perfume she had put on for *him*, Harry thought, shooting her a look that made Marnie turn and run.

As Marnie raced up the stairs to retrieve the tickets, Harry's possession seemed to chase her.

She stood in her bedroom, trying to get her breath for a moment—she didn't deserve that look!

She was looking after his kids, for God's sake, she wasn't his wife.

For Harry, the alarming thing was that it felt like it.

It felt, as he stood there pulverising the vegetables, as it might have felt if Jill had stood there dressed to the nines and wafting perfume. *I'm just going out to the ballet and for a shag afterwards, darling. Don't wait up!*

He was as angry and as defensive and as pissed off as he would have been had it been Jill clipping down the stairs. That meant something he didn't want it to mean, that it couldn't mean, because Marnie didn't want kids and family, she'd made that perfectly clear.

It was business to her.

It was supposed to be business to him—he was more than used to the nanny racing out the door on a Friday night, or their boyfriends dropping in.

He and Marnie had slept together *once*.

It was no big deal to him.

Usually.

'See you,' she called from the hall, and he heard the door open.

'See you,' he tried to call out, but the wrong words

came out. 'Could I have a word before you go?' Harry said. He nearly added, 'Young lady.'

He felt like her father as he strode down the hall.

He felt *nothing* like her father as he caught her arm and turned her round. 'Call me old-fashioned,' Harry said, 'but I'll tell you this much…I don't like this, Marnie.'

'Harry, I'm only here to help with—'

'I don't care,' Harry interrupted. 'I don't care if it's too much too soon, I don't care if you don't want to hear it, but…' He tried to stop himself, she was thirty-one, he could hardly tell her she'd be better be back here at a reasonable time, that if she slept with him…

His eyes did the talking and so did hers. Marnie was not a woman who liked to be told.

'I don't know where we're going, but there are certain things that you can't come back from,' Harry said. 'And this is one of them.'

'Oh, but it's all right for you.'

'No,' Harry said. 'You have every right to be as angry and as pissed off as I am right now if I…'

Marnie wrenched her arm from his and clipped out to the car.

Bloody men!

Sleep with them once and the next thing you know you're ironing for them, watching their kids. He'd be asking what was for dinner next!

Harry let out a few harsh breaths as he stood in the hall after she'd gone.

'Daddy?' called Charlotte.

He ignored it.

'Daddy!'

He tried to ignore it a second time.

'Daddy, what have you done to the potatoes?'

Harry walked back into the kitchen, saw the mountain of minced potatoes he'd produced and gave a wry grin as he came up with a suitable answer. 'They cook faster if they're small.'

Even Charlotte didn't seem convinced.

'Marnie looked pretty, didn't she?' Charlotte simply didn't let up. 'Is she going out with her boyfriend?'

'Charlotte.' It was Adam who fired Charlotte a warning. Perhaps it took another guy to get it, Harry thought.

What the hell was wrong with him—issuing warnings like that?

A few weeks ago, Marnie would have been the perfect woman—no strings, no commitment. Marnie had been everything he'd wanted in a woman.

He just didn't want that any more.

Marnie wasn't faring so well either.

The traffic was hell as she approached the city—there was a match on at the MCG and Marnie could cheerfully have turned round and headed for home, except she had the tickets.

She was angry with Harry for making such a big deal of things, but it felt like a big deal—she didn't want to see Matthew.

She didn't even want to see Harry.

Right now, Marnie wanted a night at home to curl up alone and try and sort out her feelings.

'Where are you?' Matthew rang and she told him she was running late and that rather than going to the hotel first she would meet him at the Arts Centre.

It was busy and there really wasn't much of a chance to talk. Marnie bought a programme and they ordered a drink and one for the interval, and then Matthew tried to make her smile. 'We could always skip the ballet and head straight to the hotel.'

And she took a breath and just said it. 'I think I might skip the hotel.'

'Marnie?'

'I need to be back by seven.' He just looked at her, nonplussed. 'I told you, I'm looking after a friend's children.'

'Who's the friend?'

'Just someone from work.'

'That was quick,' Matthew said, and Marnie sucked on her lemon. It was far sweeter than the conversation. She knew he was referring to how Marnie didn't exactly jump into friendships. 'I assume it's the doctor you were holed up in your office with.'

'Matthew, we agreed that we don't have to run every detail of our lives—'

'No, *you* decided that, you're the one who decides how much to give,' Matthew said, and Marnie could feel the people beside them briefly turn and then halt their conversations so they could listen to hers.

Matthew looked at her. 'The doctor wants a wife... Well, God help him, then,' Matthew said, 'and God help...' He halted then but Marnie knew what he'd been about to say and she challenged him.

'Meaning?'

'I never pictured you as a stepmother.'

'Oh, for the love of God.' Marnie rolled her eyes. 'I'm looking after his kids for a week.'

'Would you move in for a week to help look after mine?'

It wasn't really the time to point out that he didn't have any—even if the question was hypothetical, Marnie knew then the answer.

There'd be no Mary Poppins stopping at Matthew's door.

Even if she hadn't recognised it at the time, she had moved in because it was Harry.

When she said nothing, Matthew drained his drink. 'You're the coldest person I know, Marnie. The good doctor just hasn't worked it out yet.'

He left her standing there and Marnie wasn't about to follow.

She sipped on her drink as the bell went and people went through. She could just go home, Marnie realised, and have the evening alone she'd so desperately craved.

Shouldn't it hurt more? Marnie thought.

But it wasn't Matthew leaving that was hurting her now.

She wanted superficial. She wanted, for want of a word, relationships where it didn't feel as if you might die if the other person were to leave.

Yes, she wanted to go home, yet more than that she needed escape.

Marnie sat watching the ballet with an empty seat beside her, but not even the dancers held her mind for more than a moment. She wanted something she had never wanted before. It wasn't just Harry and giving things a go that scared her so—it was pink tights and Charlotte and the serious eyes of Adam and his wobbly tooth that had made her stomach curl, and her stomach only curled for family. Marnie was petrified—if she did try to make things work with Harry, she had to love them.

What if it didn't work?

She wouldn't lose one, she'd lose three, and Marnie truly didn't know if she could stand to lose like that again.

It was a wretched night, a long, lonely drive home,

and she was too upset to go to Harry's—she simply didn't want him to see her as confused and raw as this.

She'd feel better in the morning, Marnie assured herself as she let herself into her own home and set her alarm.

But she didn't.

'Hi.'

Harry couldn't even look at her as she let herself in at six a.m. 'I was just up with Charlotte, she should sleep for a couple more hours.' He was putting the medicine back in the cabinet and wearing only hipsters. He hadn't expected her back just yet, but more worrying than that was the effort needed to keep his voice normal, to somehow try and pretend that he hadn't said what he had last night.

Clearly, given the hour, it hadn't mattered a jot. She must have spent the night with him.

'I got a programme for Charlotte.'

'She'll love it.' Harry glanced up. There were the smudges of last night's make-up under her eyes and her hair was still curly, and his skin was alive and screaming for her, though his head denied that fact.

'About last night...' Marnie attempted. Usually she could talk, usually she found it easy to say what was on her mind, but in this she was utterly confused.

'I don't want to talk about last night,' Harry said. He was doing everything he could not to think about it.

'Matthew said—'

'Oh, so you're going to stand there quoting him now!'

She didn't want to quote Matthew, she was trying to tell him how scared she was, to warn Harry that he might be making the most terrible mistake. Marnie truly didn't know if she was capable of love. 'He said...the doctor wants a wife, and if that's the case—'

'Believe me,' Harry swiftly broke in, 'if I was on the lookout for the perfect wife…' He stopped himself. Last night's anger hadn't been dimmed by sleep—Harry had barely had any. A night spent watching the clock, a night knowing she was out and with *him*, despite the fact that he'd told her they could never come back from that!

Yes, Harry was having trouble keeping this pleasant.

'Harry, please…' Marnie walked towards him. She had never wanted the feeling of somebody else's arms around her more. She had never wanted to halt a row more, and words were failing her this morning, so she attempted a more basic form of communication—one that had always worked till now. 'I don't want to argue.'

He could smell the remnants of last night's perfume as her hand moved to his chest. His mind put it more bluntly than he chose to voice, but as her mouth moved towards his, as much as he wanted that kiss, he really didn't know where she'd been.

'It's a bit much, Marnie.' He pushed her off. 'You know, I never thought I'd say this, but I think I'm over meaningless sex.'

She went to kiss him but he moved his cheek and then he put his blunt thoughts into words

'I don't know where you've been.'

It was no surprise that she slapped him.

CHAPTER FIFTEEN

MARNIE STRIPPED OFF and pulled on her pyjamas and lay there bristling with anger, wishing Harry would just go to work, but she could hear him downstairs on the phone and then the anger faded as realisation hit.

She hadn't told him.

In all her attempts to tell him how she was feeling, she hadn't told him the one thing that he'd needed to know.

She hadn't been with Matthew.

Marnie was half expecting it when she heard the creaking stairs and then heard him walking towards her room and a soft knock before he came in.

She wished he would just leave it, yet she was glad that he didn't.

'I'm sorry.'

He handed her a mug of tea.

And he'd left the bag in!

'You should be at work.'

'I rang Helen and said I'd be in late.'

'Why?'

'To apologise. I was jealous,' Harry admitted. 'It was jealousy speaking. Just pure and simple jealousy.'

'We'd had the tickets since before—'

'I know.'

'Nothing happened. Last night.'

'Marnie, you don't have to explain yourself to me—the thing is, you don't owe me anything. It's me who owes you. And the department,' Harry added. 'The lines got blurred. Well, they did for me and I loathe what I just said.'

'Matthew and I had words as soon as we got there,' Marnie said. 'I didn't even want to go but I had the tickets. He didn't even stay for the ballet...' Marnie gave him a small smile. 'Where's Juan when you need him?'

'Sorry?'

'Instead of rowing, I could have been having a shoulder massage,' Marnie said. 'He'd be far more understanding.'

'I'm not Juan,' Harry said, and he smiled at her.

'I'm glad.'

'Though I reckon even Juan's understanding might have been pushed to the limits last night.' He looked at Marnie all rumpled in bed and that was the trouble, he liked what he saw. As naturally as breathing, Marnie moved her legs as she took a drink of her tea and Harry sat down.

'I'm confused, Harry.' She was nothing but honest as she put her mug down. 'You're the last thing I want but also the only thing I want.'

'And I feel the same about you.' He gave a half-smile and she swallowed.

'I have to love your kids?'

'Marnie...' he looked at her '...no one is asking you to suddenly love anyone.' He didn't know how best to explain it. 'You're just so closed off...' He put his hand up to her cheek and his thumb smudged a bit of last night's eyeliner away. 'You've got me rearranging you now.' He was so gentle as he told her the bit that was hurting. 'You're wonderful with them, absolutely lovely…' Then he said it, because he could—they both managed to speak their truths. 'You're just as lovely as you'd be with any patient.' He watched the wetness of a single tear fall and slither beneath the pad of his thumb. 'I just wish you'd open up a bit.'

'I don't know how.'

'I know.'

'The deal was I just looked after them,' Marnie said. 'You were the one who didn't want them getting confused.'

'Yep,' Harry agreed, 'but that deal ends on Monday.' He watched her swallow. 'If you're ever here after that, you won't be sleeping in this room. You're not a fling, Marnie, that I'm going to hide from them.'

'I'll be your girlfriend?' Marnie tried to tease, waited for him to say, as she once had to him, that he was a bit old for that, but Harry wasn't joking now.

'Yes,' Harry said, and she saw his eyes drift briefly to his ring and he addressed it. 'We've both got things that we need to sort.'

And just when Harry thought she was considering the possibility of them being together, he felt her pull back, simply retract, and he *had* to reach her.

'We've slept together once, Harry.'

'Twice.'

'Well, technically twice…' Marnie started, but his mouth was on hers and he mumbled the word into hers.

'Twice.'

He kissed first her mouth and then her face. Marnie felt the scratch of his chin on her cheek and it was sublime. He moved to her neck and lifted her hair and nuzzled at the sensitive skin as he lifted her top.

'The children…' Marnie said, as he pulled her top over her head.

'They're asleep,' Harry said, 'and they'd never come in.'

'You've made sure of that!' Marnie said, trying to keep things light, but Harry refused to be drawn. He didn't want to joke; instead, interspersed with soft, deep kisses to her stomach, he was peeling her pyjamas down her hips and then sorting out the little clothing he wore. Then he joined her, face to face, both naked.

Not for the first time.

It just felt like it as he kissed her.

Slowly, deeply, he lingered, on her mouth, her neck, her breasts, as his hand crept lower, and she moaned as his fingers stroked her. She wanted him inside her, yet she was holding him as he stroked her, forgetting to kiss, forgetting everything except the bliss of his fingers and the feel of him in her hands.

'Please,' Marnie said, guiding him to her entrance and then remembering. 'We need—'

'Not yet.'

He stroked first with his fingers and then teased her with what she wanted. Harry's hand closed around hers, both stroking him till Marnie could only marvel at his control because she was coming, just from watching him and feeling the wet velvet strokes, but even as she came he was pressing her onto her back.

'Harry.' Marnie wanted her breath back, wanted to collect her thoughts, which seemed to be dancing in the air around the bed. She felt a flail of panic as she realised she was being made love to—and Marnie didn't do that. She wanted to halt him, to stop him, to remind him how casual they were, except right here, right now, they were not. Her legs parted to him and her eyes opened to him and he waited.

He waited till she could wait no more.

'I'm on the Pill.'

It was the second time in her life she'd got carried away, but this time it wasn't a mistake.

She heard the delicious moan of relief and want as Harry moved in but his eyes didn't close.

It wasn't the absence of a condom that rendered this unprotected sex—her heart was bare and stripped and the tears she had held back last night were there in her eyes, and there was anger too for somehow he exposed her.

'Crazy about you, Marnie.' He looked at her as he said it, and she pressed her lips tighter and swallowed back the words she wanted to say, for she *was* crazy about Harry.

It was sex, Marnie told herself—so why were her eyes closing and why was her mouth demanding his? Why was she now pinned beneath him, wrapped around him? She wanted to pierce the silent morning with a scream, but on the periphery she knew they were trying to be quiet. She could hear them building, could feel Harry's back sliding beneath her fingers, and then the moment of perfect acceleration as he drove her to the edge and joined her falling.

Marnie lay there afterwards, breathing in his scent, feeling his chin in her shoulder, and she should be jumping up as she had once, gripped with panic and guilt, but beauty laced with fear silenced her for a couple of moments.

'You're not being fair on Helen.'

'I know.' He rolled off her and smiled.

'Love me and leave me,' Marnie joked, but it was a

very dangerous joke and, perhaps wisely, Harry didn't answer.

She'd be out the dodgy windows if he did.

Instead, he gave her a small kiss and climbed out of bed and, of course, there were the practicalities to discuss.

'I'll be back by eight on Monday.'

'Are they going to day care?'

'Not sure,' Harry said. 'I'll give Evelyn a call over the weekend and let you know.'

'You'll call the twins?'

'Of course,' Harry said. 'They call me all the time when I'm on take.'

She'd never worked a weekend with him.

It was a little awkward as he went to go.

'Harry?'

He turned.

'Did you remember to be a fairy last night?'

'Amazingly—yes,' Harry said. 'A very grumpy fairy.'

He wasn't grumpy now.

Marnie lay in the bath after Harry had gone to work and thought about his words earlier about the way she was with the twins.

He hadn't offended her—Harry had spoken the truth.

Yes, this last week she had looked after the twins and had a nice time with them, looked after their itches and given them their medicine. Harry was right, she gave as much of herself to them as she would to a patient.

It was all she ever gave to anyone.

How, though?

How do you open up when you don't know how?

Marnie got out of the bath and, wrapped in her dressing gown, she headed to the bedroom to dress and put on her make-up.

Her uniform, Marnie realised.

Every morning she presented herself as neatly as she would for work.

This morning, though, the very meticulous Marnie pulled back on the pyjamas Harry had so firmly discarded, combed her hair and, instead of blasting it with the hairdryer, tied it back damp.

The children were still asleep so Marnie made herself a large mug of tea and some toast and, instead of unloading the dishwasher, went and sat down and tried to relax, though it wasn't long till she heard footsteps.

'Oh!' Charlotte blinked in surprise at the sight of Marnie in pyjamas, drinking tea and looking through her ballet programme.

'I got this for you,' Marnie said.

'For me?'

'Come and have a look,' Marnie said, and Charlotte climbed onto the sofa beside her and Marnie showed her the programme and they oohed and ahhed at the costumes until Adam appeared. He showed Marnie the money the fairy had left him and then turned on the TV to watch some cartoons.

'I'd give anything to have been a ballerina,' Marnie said, getting back to the programme, looking at the gorgeous costumes she had barely taken in last night.

'You could change jobs,' Charlotte suggested.

Marnie laughed at Charlotte's simplicity. 'I think I've left it a bit late.'

'Were you good at ballet?' Charlotte asked.

'I've never done it,' Marnie said. 'I did Irish dancing.'

'What's that?'

'Irish dancing,' Marnie said, as Charlotte sat there nonplussed, and then Marnie did something she never did, or hadn't in what felt like for ever. 'I'll show you.'

The sound of Charlotte laughing and Adam joining in too made Marnie dance faster.

'Stop.' Charlotte was standing on the couch, both crying and laughing; Adam was curled up, laughing too.

'I haven't got to the really fast bit yet.'

It was *their* day.

They made a tiny miniature feast for the fairies and had their own picnic in the living room—Marnie opened the French doors and let the sun stream in as they sat on a blanket and pretended they were in a field.

Harry rang that evening to say goodnight but Marnie made sure she was busy upstairs, blushing a bit at the memory of the morning, still feeling a little as if she was playing house.

'Can we put more food out for the fairies tomorrow?' Charlotte said, but Marnie shook her head.

'They'll be too fat to fly if we keep feeding them. Now, you get some sleep.' She gave Charlotte a smile and headed out of her room and then into Adam's.

''Night, Marnie.'

'Would you like a story?' Marnie said because, unlike Charlotte, Adam never really asked for anything, and she smiled when he nodded.

It was a slightly different version of the one she had told Charlotte, and her nieces and nephews and brothers, but it was lovely to see Adam smiling and asking questions, though not as many as Charlotte had.

'Are we going back to day care on Monday?'

'I think so.' Marnie smiled but it faded after she had turned out the light and closed the door and realised this could well be her second-last night at the house.

Charlotte had the same question the next day after lunch. As she seemed a little bit tired and tearful, Marnie had suggested she have a little sleep, but it had been met by scorn.

'I don't need a sleep.' She looked at Marnie and made a quick amendment. 'Though I still don't feel well,' she added hurriedly. 'When do we go back to day care?'

'I'm not sure,' Marnie admitted. 'I think Daddy was going to call Evelyn over the weekend.'

'I'm going to ring him,' Charlotte said, but was upset a few minutes later when she came back into the lounge. 'Daddy can't come to the phone.'

'He's just busy,' Marnie said, because she'd just been watching the news. There had been an emergency in the city and now a pile-up more locally. 'He'll call you back as soon as he can.'

Even though there was nothing she could do to help, Marnie still called Emergency and spoke with Kelly.

'We're a bit snowed under,' Kelly said. 'But we're coping. Thankfully it happened just after the late staff came on, so there were plenty of us.'

Yes, there were plenty of nurses but as Harry examined a potential spinal injury, he wished there were a few more consultants.

An eighteen-year-old who had got his driving licence on Friday had taken a friend out and met up another newly licensed friend.

And his friend!

Harry had seen it and heard it and dealt with it more times than he should be able to remember.

Yet he remembered each one.

The trauma team had taken the first driver straight to Theatre and Harry was dealing with the passenger, who, though conscious, was displaying worrying signs. 'Squeeze my hands,' Harry said, and the patient did so. 'Okay, try and lift your left leg…'

'I can't.'

'Okay. Can you wiggle your toes for me?'

'Harry!' He could hear Kelly calling him from be-hind the curtain. 'Harry, now, please!'

He needed two of him.

'You paged the second on trauma?' Harry checked with Miriam, who nodded. 'Fast-page them again,' Harry said, and quickly gave Sheldon some instructions.

'Harry!' Kelly was calling him again as he stepped in. 'He's not responding...'

'Carl!' Harry pinched the young man's ear; he had been talking just a few minutes ago when Harry had been called for the spinal injury. When pinching his ear failed to elicit a response Harry tried a sternal rub. 'Carl!' Harry ran his pen over the young man's nail bed and watched as he extended to pain.

'Start some mannitol,' Harry said, prescribing an IV solution to reduce intracranial pressure. 'Let's him round for an MRI.'

'Are you going with him?' Kelly checked, and just as Harry was coming to an impossible decision, just as he heard the roar of the storm become louder, a deep accented voice brought calm.

'Can I help?'

'Juan!'

'I heard on the radio that there had been a big acci-dent. I thought you and Dr Vermont might need a hand.'

There wasn't time for conversation, let alone to break the terrible news. 'I've got a query spinal in the next curtain who I'm very concerned about...'

'I've got it.'

For Harry there was almost a feeling of dizziness—it was such a relief to know that Juan was back, that there was another consultant to share the load, to know that he didn't have to think about the young man in the next bed—he was getting the best of care from Juan. Harry could focus now on Carl.

The afternoon passed in a blur of MRIs and transfers, but later, as Juan returned from Theatre, where his patient had been taken for halo traction, he caught Harry as he came off the phone.

'So, is he playing golf?'

'Sorry?'

'Dr Vermont.' Juan rolled his eyes because Dr Vermont did love his golf at weekends, or rather had.

'Juan…' There was no one critical now, it was time to tell him properly before he heard it in passing. He asked Juan if he could have a word in his office and once there Harry closed the door. 'Dr Vermont passed away.' He saw the shock on his colleague's face. Even though Juan was fairly new to the department, it was still a terrible shock. 'He was doing a night shift and suffered a massive myocardial infarction.'

'Who was on?'

'Sheldon,' Harry said. 'And Eric was the cardiologist. They did everything they could, of course. He was having supper with Marnie in her office and just…' Harry shook his head and gave a weary shrug.

'Poor Marnie.'

'Yep,' Harry said. 'She got help, she did everything right, but there was nothing to be done.'

Juan was stunned. He asked about Marjorie. 'They were having their fortieth wedding anniversary.'

'They had it,' Harry said. 'It was after that.'

'So how have you managed?' Juan asked.

'Barely,' Harry said. 'Juan, there's something else I ought to tell you—I handed my notice in a few days before Dr Vermont died. The twins have both had chickenpox, something had to give. Oh….' he gave a wry laugh '…and my babysitter got shingles.'

'So you're leaving?'

'I don't know,' Harry admitted. 'Now that you're back, hopefully things will be better, but I need to put the children more to the front than the back of the queue. Speaking of which…' he grimaced when he saw the time '…I was supposed to call Charlotte.'

'Go home,' Juan said.

'You're not due back till tomorrow..'

'What did you just say about putting your priorities in order?' Juan checked. 'Go and spend the evening with your children.'

Harry smiled. It was so good to have Juan back. 'How was the wedding?'

'Amazing. I will tell you about it properly later. Right now I am going to call Cate and let her know I am here for the night.'

'Thanks.'

'Who's been helping with the children?' Juan asked.

'They've been here there and everywhere,' Harry said, which was in part the truth. It had only been since Marnie had stepped in that things had been so stable, but certainly Marnie didn't want anyone knowing she had temporarily moved in.

Temporarily.

Marnie was starting to sort out her case, and was just putting Declan's photo in when there was a knock at the front door and she opened it to a lady who introduced herself as Evelyn. 'Harry rang me last night and told me the twins had been sick.'

'I'm Marnie,' she said. 'A colleague of Harry's. I've been watching the twins over the weekend while he's been working.' It was easier than saying she'd been here for a week.

'Evelyn!' Charlotte came charging down the stairs.

'Charlotte! I've missed you so much!' Evelyn was so effusive and loving and the children ran to her. 'I was so upset to hear you'd got chickenpox.' As she hugged the twins Evelyn looked over to Marnie. 'If I'd known I was infectious, I'd have stayed well away.'

'They're fine,' Marnie said.

'Poor Harry, how on earth did he manage?'

'It's been a bit of a juggle but he got there.'

'Well, I can help now.' Evelyn was clearly at home here. While she chatted to Charlotte, who was filling her in on every detail of her spots, Evelyn was filling the kettle.

Charlotte was so thrilled to see her that when Marnie's phone rang, Charlotte barely looked over as Marnie excused herself and headed upstairs. She was feeling horribly rattled and suddenly entirely replaceable.

'Hi, Mum.' Marnie did her best to sound cheerful, not that Maureen appreciated the effort.

'I know you're busy, Marnie, but it's been more than a month since you visited.'

'I know, Mum.'

'Well, on Thursday Ronan has his hand appointment. I was thinking, your father and I could bring him and then, when you've finished work, we could go out for dinner.'

Was she serious? Thursday was Declan's birthday.

'Ronan said you liked the prawns at the pub—'

'Mum.'

'And your dad loves a nice steak.'

'Mum!' Marnie picked up Declan's photo from the case—did her mother really think she wanted to be sitting eating prawns and talking about the bloody weather? 'I've got plans that day.'

'I know you do, Marnie, but, I think it would be nice if we could all be together.'

'I told you, I'm busy.'

She turned off the phone and stared at Declan.

Her son.

Did her mum really think they could get through the night of his birthday not talking about him?

Avoiding his memory and the terrible hurt.

Guilt filled Marnie as she looked at a photo that had been placed in a drawer while she'd played houses, looking after someone else's children, telling fairy tales that, yes, she'd once told Declan, even if he'd been far too young to understand them.

A part of her knew her guilt was misplaced, but this was her hardest time. She wanted it to be the week after next when she was over the hurdle of Declan's birthday.

But a fortnight from then it would be the anniversary of his death.

It never entered her head she could share her pain.

Oh, God, tears were filling her eyes but, as she was fast finding out, there was no such thing as suitable quiet time with a house of four-year-olds. She could hear Charlotte racing up the stairs, calling her name.

'Marnie!'

'I'll be there in a minute.'

'Daddy's home!'

Marnie headed downstairs to find Charlotte telling Harry about their weekend as Evelyn looked on happily.

'The fairies came and ate the food we left them...'

'Wow!' Harry said, but she could see it was all a bit forced. Still, he made plans for tomorrow with Evelyn and once she was gone and Charlotte was upstairs, Harry let out a sigh of relief.

'How was it?' Marnie asked.

'Grim,' Harry admitted. 'Juan's there now. I can't tell you how good it felt to hand the lot over to him.' He glanced at the television that was on in the background, the news regaling them with details of the accident. 'Who'd have teenagers?' Harry said, and looked over at Adam as Marnie busied herself wiping the bench down, terrified she might break down, because right now she'd give anything to have one. 'I've got it all to come,' Harry said.

'We'll be good.' Adam smiled.

'That's what they all say!'

'Can you read me a story?' Charlotte was walking in with a book. 'Mummy, can you—?'

'Marnie!' She snapped a little more than she'd intended. 'It's Marnie,' she said again, and Charlotte's cheeks went very pink and she turned and ran off.

'Adam,' Harry said, 'go and help Charlotte choose a story and I'll be in.' As Adam walked off he turned to her. 'It was a simple mistake,' Harry said. 'She's four.'

'I know,' Marnie said. 'I just…' She couldn't explain it properly, the little reference to teenagers, hearing Charlotte call her Mummy—it hurt and it hurt and it hurt and she wanted the hurt to stop. 'I'm not going to have her call me Mummy and get all confused.'

'Sure.'

'Harry, I think I ought to go,' Marnie said, and Harry stood silent. 'I've got so much to do at home…'

She was back to being the babysitter and there was nothing Harry could do.

'Stay for dinner?'

'I'd rather not. I'm ready for home.' She gave him a tight smile. 'I'll go and speak to the children.'

She was terribly nice to them.

Harry stood at the door as she said goodbye to Charlotte and told her she was sorry for snapping.

'Some things make me sad.'

'Like what?'

'Like—' Marnie was as honest as she could be with a four-year-old '—I don't have children.'

'You said you didn't want babies.'

'Well, most of the time I feel like that,' Marnie said. 'Just not all the time.'

Harry hadn't seen her with the children over the weekend. He watched as she was very kind and very honest with the twins...but, yes, she held back. 'I'm going to go back to my house now,' Marnie said. 'Dr Juan starts tomorrow, your spots are all gone...'

'Will we see you again?'

'Of course!' Marnie said. 'I'm sure you'll be dropping in to the department.'

It wasn't what they wanted, though.

They got their first and last kiss from Marnie.

Just a brief one.

She didn't want them, Harry realised.

Which meant she didn't want him.

'Thank you.' Harry helped her take her stuff out to the car.

'It's been great,' Marnie said, and then she sent their relationship straight back to where it had started. 'Not that we'll be telling anyone at work about it.'

'Of course.'

'If I had an umbrella I'd put it up!'

He couldn't even smile at her pale joke.

'Next week,' Harry said, 'once Juan's back, I'd like to take you out to dinner to properly say thank you.'

'There's no need for that.'

No, she could not have made it clearer.

'I really am grateful,' Harry said, remembering the reason Marnie had been there.

The only reason.

Work.

'We got through it,' he said.

'We did!' Marnie smiled. 'Two consultants and another soon starting! We'll be back on track in no time.'

CHAPTER SIXTEEN

IT REALLY WAS business as usual.

At work at least.

The house had been as cold as a morgue after she'd gone.

It was strange, because there were always nannies and aunts and people coming and going, but without Marnie it felt like some sinkhole had opened up and plunged them back into darkness.

'I love Marnie...' Charlotte was crying.

'Charlotte!' He'd been about to tell her she was too dramatic, but she did love her, Harry realised, and Adam did too, because Harry could hear him crying in his bedroom. 'Marnie adores you.'

'Then why isn't she here?'

It was one question he couldn't answer.

He wanted to remind the twins she'd only been there for a few days, yet by the end of a week without Marnie—near midnight on the Sunday night—Harry had done what he'd thought he'd never be ready to do and taken his ring off.

He loved Jill so much but it felt wrong to be wearing it when he was mourning someone else.

All he knew now was that being in bed with Marnie was amazing, but more than that, when she laughed, when she smiled, or when her honesty was so breath-taking your biscuit snapped in mid-dunk, Harry wanted more.

But Marnie didn't want intimacy.

Marnie didn't want them.

You had to admire her really.

Harry sat at work, late afternoon on the Wednesday, trying to write, trying not to turn to the sound of her voice.

'Did you forget how to use surgical taps when you were on your honeymoon?' Like a hawk swooping, she was off her stool and straight onto Juan. 'I'll remind you how to use them, Juan.'

'Marnie, I'm not about to see a patient...'

'It's about good habits,' Marnie said. 'Which means if you use the surgical sink then you're to use it as such and turn it off with your elbows.' She was demonstrating again and Juan was grinning.

'Show me again, Marnie,' Juan said.

Harry could stand it no longer and anyway he had somewhere he needed to be. In an attempt to cheer Charlotte he'd rung up about ballet lessons and she had her first one at five. 'Got to go,' Harry said.

'Before you do I need you to witness my signature.' Juan had an interview with Immigration the next day about getting permanent residence in Australia. 'For the immigration forms...'

'No problem,' Harry said. 'I need to get Charlotte changed here anyway. I'll just go and get them and, if you can have everything ready, I'll sign them on my way out.'

Marnie didn't hide in her office, neither did she disappear, but she was glad she was with a patient as she heard Charlotte's excited chatter from behind a curtain a little later.

'I want to show Marnie.'

'She's busy,' Harry said. 'Come on.'

'But I want her to see—'

'We'll be late,' Harry said.

She waited just a moment before walking out, relieved that they'd gone, but then Harry dashed back.

'You've pocketed my pen,' Harry said to Juan, who was always borrowing things and forgetting to give them back. 'I was just—'

'Marnie!' Charlotte was running behind him. 'Look!'

She had on pink ballet tights and a pink headband and she looked so gorgeous and excited that Marnie wanted to drop to her knees. She wanted to tuck in her curls under the headband and to tie her cardigan properly, because Harry's attempt at a bow was already unravelling, but she just stood and smiled as Charlotte spoke. 'I've got my first ballet lesson.'

'Good toes, naughty toes,' Marnie said. 'Have a wonderful time.'

She said everything right, Harry thought, and she smiled as she did, but it was like watching the security screen shoot up at the bank, he thought as Marnie stepped forward then halted.

'Come on, Charlotte,' Harry said. 'You don't want to be late.'

Marnie stood watching as Harry took his children's hands and walked off, and he didn't look back—his priority was his children.

No matter the cost.

She felt Juan watching her and turned quickly, taking out an alcohol wipe to clean down the bench. 'That'll be you before you know it,' Marnie said, trying to make conversation, embarrassed to have been caught watching Harry and the twins. 'Dashing off to take your little ones to their activities.'

'I hope so,' Juan said, and got back to his work. Marnie just stood there cleaning, hating how easy and honest his answer had been—that Juan could admit his hopes for the future, that he wasn't whipping out an alcohol wipe and cleaning something that didn't even need to be cleaned.

'Marnie—' Juan started, perhaps sensing her sudden distress.

'Don't!' Marnie snapped, and walked briskly to her office. She didn't want Juan waving his fairy dust on her and giving her one of his, oh, so meaningful talks.

Oh, she couldn't deal with this today.

Or tomorrow.

Especially tomorrow.

CHAPTER SEVENTEEN

'Hi, Juan!' Charlotte was still practising her dance moves when Juan arrived unexpectedly. She was sitting on the floor and doing good toes, naughty toes.

'Marnie said that's what we'd do!' she said to Harry, and Juan saw his colleague's jaw tense and knew that he was right.

'Sorry to drop in,' Juan said. 'I messed up the form.'

'It looked fine to me.'

'I had to do it again.'

Harry wasn't in the mood for conversation, though Juan was chatting about work—Helen was covering tonight and considering a permanent position. He witnessed Juan's signature again but tensed when he still hung around. 'I'd invite you for dinner but it's nuggets and tinned spaghetti…' As he served up dinner, Harry turned briefly to Juan. 'Don't you have a new wife to get home to? You're barely back from your honeymoon.'

'At least we had one. I hear Marnie was going to ring and try to haul me back.'

Her name was everywhere.

'Yes, well, it worked out without her having to.'

'She wouldn't have had much luck, anyway.' Juan shrugged. 'I turned off my phone.'

'Wouldn't that be nice?' Harry said, taking the children's dinner over and calling them to the table.

'How did you manage?' Juan, oh, so casually asked.

'Marnie looked after us,' Charlotte said, as Harry poured the twins drinks.

Harry's smile was wry as he ruffled Charlotte's hair.

'I'll see you out,' Harry said. He needed to be on his own with his children right now.

'Harry,' Juan said. Since his return he'd been worried about Harry. Juan had thought it was grief and from the look of his friend it was, yet it wasn't just Dr Vermont he was grieving for. 'If you want to talk—'

'I don't,' Harry broke in, though he'd love to open up to someone who had been out there a bit more recently, to discuss how the hell this friends-with-benefits thing worked, or just the hell of loving someone who didn't want love.

Yes, he loved her.

And because he loved her, he knew Marnie would loathe it to be discussed. She would hate Juan, and therefore Cate, knowing what had briefly gone on between them.

So he said nothing—he just wished Juan good luck with Immigration tomorrow.

'I should be back by midday.'

'No problem,' Harry said.

He was glad that everyone wasn't rushing to get to the department, that finally there was some calm to the place.

Just not to his heart.

'What time's hand clinic?' Kelly asked.

'Three,' Harry answered.

'I'm going to go and set up while it's quiet.'

Harry said nothing. He was past multi-tasking—just filling out a doctor's letter was taking all his concentration. Marnie was holed up in her office and Harry would love to do the same, except Juan wasn't back yet from Immigration.

'I'm here to see Marnie Johnson.' Harry glanced up as Kelly asked a man in a suit if she could help him.

Perhaps it was one of her brothers, Harry attempted, but he didn't have an Irish accent.

It had nothing to do with him, Harry told himself and carried on writing as Kelly buzzed Marnie and she came through to the department.

'Craig.' He heard Marnie's voice and deliberately didn't look up. 'I said to text when you were here and I'd meet you outside. Kelly, I'm going to be away from the department for my lunch break.'

Now, as she walked away, Harry did look up.

There was a wedding ring on Craig's finger. Harry could see it as he put his arm around Marnie's shoulders, but unlike with Matthew she didn't wriggle away.

Instead, Harry watched as her hand moved up to catch his.

Did she have to rub his face in it? Harry thought.

Was she so cold she could nip off to lunch with a married man and not care who knew?

Even him?

Yes.

It got worse as he took his lunch break.

'Guess who got picked up by a man and has now rung in with a sudden migraine?' Kelly smirked as she plonked herself down and opened her sandwich.

'Oh, but she'd have something to say if we did it,' Abby bristled.

But there was no Dr Vermont to say 'Ladies,' so Harry had to sit through it.

It was a relief to go back to work.

For ten minutes.

'Ronan.' Harry forced a smile as yet another reminder of Marnie came through. 'How are you?'

'Nervous,' Ronan admitted, as Harry carefully took the splint off and examined his finger for sensation.

'I couldn't be happier with it,' Harry said. 'It's going to take time to get back full range and function...'

'I know.'

'But for now everything looks better than I'd expected. Keep the splint on and I'll see you again in two weeks, but you can start now with the hand therapist.' He couldn't not mention her. 'Marnie is—'

'Oh, no, don't disturb her,' Ronan interrupted and shook his head and Harry frowned because it sounded as if Ronan was avoiding her.

'I was just about to say I'd let her know you were here, but she's actually off sick.'

'Okay.' Ronan stood and, although he was usually articulate and friendly, he didn't express concern or say that he knew; instead, he was suddenly awkward and Harry watched as Ronan shrugged and blushed and then shook Harry's hand.

Harry knew.

He knew then what day it was today—the day the Johnsons always avoided each other, the day that no one could discuss.

'Don't bring the next one in.' Harry halted Kelly and buzzed through to the main section. 'Is Juan back yet?'

'He's just getting something to eat before he starts,' Miriam answered, but Harry had other ideas.

He found him in the kitchen.

'Juan, can you take over hand clinic? I need to go.'

'Now?'

'Now.'

He just walked away from hand clinic, from Emergency, from all of it, without a backward glance and went to his car.

He drove to her street. If there was a car outside then he'd just keep going and come back later, but he guessed that there wouldn't be—Harry knew she would get through it and then want to be alone.

She didn't have to be.

That much he knew.

'Marnie...' He knocked and she didn't answer, so he knocked again. 'I'm not going till you open the door.'

'Make yourself comfortable on the doorstep,' came the smart answer.

'I know that it's Declan's birthday.'

There was no movement for a moment but then the door opened. Marnie looked as if she did have a migraine. Her already pale face was a chalky white and her eyes were glittering more with pain than tears.

'I don't talk about it.'

'But you can.'

He took her in his arms.

'I don't know how to,' she admitted, because it was easier to sob into a phone to Siobhan and then end the call when it got too hard.

'We'll work it out.'

'I've just been to the cemetery,' Marnie explained. 'I couldn't face coming back to work. Craig, that's his father, well, we don't go every year, sometimes he's away with work, but this year we went together. His wife's pregnant with their third...' She looked up at Harry.

'I am pleased for him and there's nothing like that between us, it's just…'

'Hard?'

'Not all the time,' Marnie admitted, 'but this birthday has been a bad one. He'd have been a teenager today.'

'I'm so sorry.' He still held her in his arms.

'I'd have a thirteen-year-old and be dealing with acne and rebellion and dirty bedrooms.' She leant on him. 'I want him to be thirteen.'

'I know.'

Harry did know. He knew about impossible wishes and guilt, because if his wish for Jill had come true, then he wouldn't be here with Marnie.

But he wanted to be here.

Especially now that she let him be.

She cried and she cried and he held her and then she cried for other things.

'I'm sorry I snapped at Charlotte.'

'Forget it.'

'I can't.'

'She loves you. Adam loves you.' He looked at her. 'I love you.'

'I'm so scared,' Marnie said. 'I'm so scared to fall in love and to love and—'

'You don't have a choice,' Harry said. 'In case you hadn't noticed, love doesn't let you choose. If it did, you'd be an amazing cook, a stay-at-home kind of woman…'

'You'd be bored.'

'I know.' Harry smiled. 'And you wouldn't have chosen a single father.'

'How do you know that?'

'You told me,' Harry said. 'Several times.'

'I didn't choose a single father,' Marnie said. 'I

chose you and your children…' She thought of Adam so guarded and Charlotte so dazzling. 'They chose me.'

And on a day when she ached for her own son, there was room too for his, because a while later she found herself talking about another child who had wormed his way to her heart. 'Adam doesn't have a speech problem,' Marnie said, as she drank yet another mug of tea that Harry had made her. 'He's got the same problem that Ronan had—an older sister who says everything for him.'

'Perhaps.'

'No perhaps about it,' Marnie said, and just as she was almost smiling, Harry changed her world.

'Come home.'

'Not like this.' Marnie crumpled, terrified at the final hurdle. 'I can't go there all sad.' She used his trump card. 'It will confuse them.'

'Do you think they've never been sad?' Harry asked.

'Of course they have.'

'So let us take care of you today.'

Marnie didn't know how to have her heart taken care of, Harry realised. She was an expert in every department but that one.

He packed her overnight bag and led her to his car, and in no time they were back at Harry's.

'You can't tell them about Declan…'

'Come on.' Harry took her hand and led her up the path and he saw their little worried faces as Marnie came in and it was clear that she had been crying.

'Hi.' Marnie stood there shy and awkward as Harry had a word to Evelyn, who made herself scarce.

'I'll be over in the morning,' Evelyn called.

'Thanks, Evelyn,' Harry said, and then led Marnie to the lounge.

'Okay.' He looked at the twins. 'You know how you feel sad about Mum sometimes?'

Charlotte nodded.

'How I feel sad sometimes?' Harry checked. 'Well, that's how Marnie feels today. I'm going to go and run her a bath and then make something to eat, so for now can you guys look after her?'

He left them to it.

'Sorry I was mean, Charlotte,' Marnie said.

'That's okay,' Charlotte said.

'You can call me whatever you want,' Marnie said. 'Well, so long as you remember Miss Manners.' She smiled and so too did Charlotte, but then Marnie stopped smiling and she wanted to turn and run because tears were threatening, but instead of running she sat down.

There was one good thing about grief, they knew what to do. Adam climbed on her knee and hugged her and she hugged him back and buried her face in his hair and just held him.

'Sorry,' Marnie said as she started to cry.

'Don't be sorry,' Charlotte said, and cuddled her too, and the twins were like little grown-ups and babies at the same time; they had been through so much and therefore could give so much.

Harry came in a little while later to find his three favourite people all cuddled in on the couch.

'Your bath's ready.' He took her hand and led her up the stairs and told the twins to wait there. Harry was so careful not to flaunt anything in front of the children but as natural as breathing he led Marnie up to the bathroom. There were bubbles and towels and not a hint of anything but love in the room as he helped her out of her clothes and into the warm bath and then left her.

'Is she okay?' Adam checked.

'She will be,' Harry said, and they headed to the kitchen to sort out something for Marnie to eat.

'Did her husband die?' Adam asked, as they loaded a tray.

'No,' Harry said.

'Her baby died,' Charlotte whispered. She was far too wise. 'I saw the photo...'

'Yes,' Harry said. 'Marnie's baby died a long time ago but it still hurts. Today would have been Declan's birthday.'

'We could make him a cake.'

'Charlotte!' Harry warned, and then almost dropped the kettle when he heard Marnie's voice and realised that she must have heard that little gem. 'She didn't mean—'

'It's fine.' Marnie smiled and gave a very worried-looking Charlotte a hug. 'It's a lovely thought but right now I'm so tired.'

'Go to bed,' Harry said. 'We'll bring this up.'

They headed upstairs together and Marnie went to turn left for her old bedroom, because surely it was too soon to do otherwise?

But it wasn't too soon. It was now.

'This way,' Harry said, and she stepped into her new bedroom. And was there any nicer way to be installed in your new bed than to have a very excited Charlotte pulling back the cover and Adam waiting with a tray? It was normal, it was natural, and it was the nicest way it could have happened.

'Okay,' Harry said, sending the twins away and pulling the curtains and putting on the bedside lamp. 'Have something to eat and a rest.' He looked at her glittering eyes and it was a relief to sit down on the bed and to take one beautiful hand in his and hold it as he perhaps said the entirely wrong thing.

'Why don't you ring your mum?' He held on tight to her hand as she pulled away. 'You need your mum.'

And her mum needed her too.

'My battery's flat.'

'There's a phone by the bed.'

An hour or so later Harry had got the children to bed when he heard the click of the phone, and then he heard the tears and the murmurs of conversation as Maureen got her wish.

'If I could take back one day in my life...' Maureen said. 'I know you can never forgive me.'

Marnie closed her eyes but not in anger.

'I do, though,' Marnie said. 'I know you were just angry.'

'I'd have loved him, though, Marnie. I was so cross but I'd bought a little coat for him and I was looking at cots. I was brought up in a world where the worst thing was your daughter getting pregnant, but it wasn't the worse thing, it was losing Declan and losing you...'

'I'm here, Mum.'

'I'm proud of you, Marnie. I know I didn't act as if I was then. Have you been to the cemetery?'

'With Craig,' Marnie said.

Yes, Marnie had chosen well.

She had a son.

He had a father—that foolish mistake wasn't so foolish all these years on.

That Declan was buried in Australia had been the only thing that had kept her here at times, but now, finally, she knew the reason she was here. Finally she felt at home.

'Let me come over. I don't want you to be on your own.' Gushing in, high on maternal waves, Maureen wanted to be with her child, but when Marnie said no, this time it wasn't because she was avoiding her.

'I'm with someone, Mum.'

'Craig?'

'No.' She looked around the bedroom, a room she'd never so much as kissed Harry in, but she could feel the love.

'His name's Harry and he's got twins.'

'Twins!'

'Their names and Charlotte and Adam,' Marnie said. 'You'll get to meet them soon. Harry's a consultant where I work.'

Maureen sat silent for a moment as Marnie opened the doors to all the separate compartments of her life and finally let her mother in.

'It sounds as if the two of you are serious.'

She wasn't serious, though.

Marnie was happy.

As he crept in the room later, trying not to disturb her, Marnie watched as he undressed, and then Harry saw the glitter of her eyes in the darkness. 'You're awake!'

'Very.'

Oh, it was lovely to feel him climb into bed and lie there beside her, and Harry lay wondering what to say to her.

Or if they might…

No, not tonight, Harry told himself.

'Are you just going to lie there?' Marnie asked, and Harry found himself laughing. 'I told my mother we were serious,' Marnie warned him, 'so you'll have to marry me now.'

'Done.'

'On one condition.' They turned to face each other. 'We're keeping this house.'

'Marnie,' Harry warned, 'we'll be buried under renovations.'

'I don't care.'

'Can we talk about this another time?' Harry said, because their legs were twining around each other's.

'I like to know what's happening,' Marnie said. 'I like things organised.'

And he knew then he had her for ever.

'Yes, Marnie, we'll keep the house.' Harry smiled as he kissed her.

Marnie had found her home.

EPILOGUE

'I SWEAR THAT she is.'

Kelly took off her shoes and stretched her feet. 'Her dress is too tight and she never takes that jacket off.'

Harry just smiled to himself and carried on watching the television.

'Her boobs are bigger,' Kelly went on. '*And* she's being nice. I've got the next four Saturdays off.'

'Marnie doesn't do nice,' Abby grumbled, because Marnie had just given her a long talking to about being consistently late, which, of course, Marnie never was.

Not once.

'She's so cold that if she is pregnant she'll lay her eggs in a river—'

'Hey!' Juan said, because Juan liked Marnie and the way she ran the place.

Harry just smiled.

Juan had an inkling but the rest of them had no clue, and that was the way Marnie had wanted it. She was determined to prove, before everyone found out, that they could work together and argue and clash at times, and Harry certainly got no favours.

At work.

Marnie was twenty weeks pregnant, and everything was going perfectly. The children were besotted with her

and called her Marmie—a mixture of Mummy and Marnie—and it was their own in-joke. Marnie had found a
day-care centre near their home rather than in the hospital. It was one Evelyn could walk to if Harry or Marnie couldn't get there, but that happened rarely. Marnie
took her management days at home and the occasional
sick day too, and somehow they had a routine and the
children were absolutely thriving

Charlotte was doing ballet; Adam was desperate to
be an older brother. They had put in an offer on the
house, even though it needed a demolition ball. Marnie
had listed every single thing that needed repairing and
read off the list to a very weary Dave, several times,
until finally their offer was accepted.

Marnie came in and opened her salad and stirred in
the dressing, just as she always did.

She was still slim, but even with her jacket on it was
getting more obvious with each passing day and she
really needed to speak to Cate about filling in for her
when she went on maternity leave.

'I'm sure you've all heard the rumours,' Marnie said,
and Kelly gave a triumphant eye-raise. 'And they're correct. I'm getting married next Saturday.'

'Marnie!' Juan came over and Marnie stood as he
gave her a kiss to congratulate her, and so too did his
wife, Cate.

'Oh!' Cate looked at the engagement ring on Marnie's finger. 'That's beautiful.'

'I know,' Marnie said. 'I'm just wearing it to show
you. I'll be taking it off at the end of lunch break.'

Cate suppressed a smile. Marnie *loathed* anything
other than the simplest of jewellery, lest there be a germ
beneath it.

Marnie looked down at her beautiful hand and even

more beautiful ring, and it made her so happy that she couldn't help smiling.

'And, yes...' her cheeks were a bit pink as she told her colleagues what they probably already knew '...I'm expecting.'

'I'm thrilled for you, Marnie,' Juan said.

'I'm thrilled for myself,' Marnie said. 'Now, it's just a small wedding, well, as small as it can be with my massive family, but you're all very welcome to come—all very informal but there'll be a good party after.'

'I didn't know you were seeing anyone,' Abby fished.

'I don't bring my personal life to work,' Marnie said.

'Will you be changing your name?' Kelly asked.

'No.' Marnie shook her head. 'It would be too confusing.'

'Confusing?'

'Marnie Worthington,' she said. 'I think having the consultant and the manager with the same surname...'

'You mean...?' They all looked at Harry, who smiled back at them, and although they never usually showed affection at work, in this instance, he reached out and pulled his soon-to-be wife onto his knee.

'I'm very disappointed in all of you,' Harry said. 'I can't believe that you didn't work it out sooner.'

Harry watched as Abby's cheeks went purple as she remembered her little reptilian comment earlier, but he just smiled back at her.

Harry couldn't stop smiling.

He loved it that no one could quite work out Marnie, not even he at times.

But he'd spend the rest of his life trying.

'Harry?' Juan went over, his smile never wider, and,

because it was Juan, he wrapped Harry and Marnie in a hug. 'This is wonderful, unexpected, amazing...'

'I know,' Harry said. 'Like Marnie.'

* * * * *

Mills & Boon® Hardback

February 2014

ROMANCE

MEDICAL

0114GEN STD HB

Mills & Boon® Large Print

February 2014

ROMANCE

The Greek's Marriage Bargain	Sharon Kendrick
An Enticing Debt to Pay	Annie West
The Playboy of Puerto Banús	Carol Marinelli
Marriage Made of Secrets	Maya Blake
Never Underestimate a Caffarelli	Melanie Milburne
The Divorce Party	Jennifer Hayward
A Hint of Scandal	Tara Pammi
Single Dad's Christmas Miracle	Susan Meier
Snowbound with the Soldier	Jennifer Faye
The Redemption of Rico D'Angelo	Michelle Douglas
Blame It on the Champagne	Nina Harrington

HISTORICAL

A Date with Dishonour	Mary Brendan
The Master of Stonegrave Hall	Helen Dickson
Engagement of Convenience	Georgie Lee
Defiant in the Viking's Bed	Joanna Fulford
The Adventurer's Bride	June Francis

MEDICAL

Miracle on Kaimotu Island	Marion Lennox
Always the Hero	Alison Roberts
The Maverick Doctor and Miss Prim	Scarlet Wilson
About That Night...	Scarlet Wilson
Daring to Date Dr Celebrity	Emily Forbes
Resisting the New Doc In Town	Lucy Clark

Mills & Boon® Hardback
March 2014

ROMANCE

A Prize Beyond Jewels	Carole Mortimer
A Queen for the Taking?	Kate Hewitt
Pretender to the Throne	Maisey Yates
An Exception to His Rule	Lindsay Armstrong
The Sheikh's Last Seduction	Jennie Lucas
Enthralled by Moretti	Cathy Williams
The Woman Sent to Tame Him	Victoria Parker
What a Sicilian Husband Wants	Michelle Smart
Waking Up Pregnant	Mira Lyn Kelly
Holiday with a Stranger	Christy McKellen
The Returning Hero	Soraya Lane
Road Trip With the Eligible Bachelor	Michelle Douglas
Safe in the Tycoon's Arms	Jennifer Faye
Awakened By His Touch	Nikki Logan
The Plus-One Agreement	Charlotte Phillips
For His Eyes Only	Liz Fielding
Uncovering Her Secrets	Amalie Berlin
Unlocking the Doctor's Heart	Susanne Hampton

MEDICAL

Waves of Temptation	Marion Lennox
Risk of a Lifetime	Caroline Anderson
To Play with Fire	Tina Beckett
The Dangers of Dating Dr Carvalho	Tina Beckett

0214GEN STD HB

ROMANCE

Million Dollar Christmas Proposal	Lucy Monroe
A Dangerous Solace	Lucy Ellis
The Consequences of That Night	Jennie Lucas
Secrets of a Powerful Man	Chantelle Shaw
Never Gamble with a Caffarelli	Melanie Milburne
Visconti's Forgotten Heir	Elizabeth Power
A Touch of Temptation	Tara Pammi
A Little Bit of Holiday Magic	Melissa McClone
A Cadence Creek Christmas	Donna Alward
His Until Midnight	Nikki Logan
The One She Was Warned About	Shoma Narayanan

HISTORICAL

Rumours that Ruined a Lady	Marguerite Kaye
The Major's Guarded Heart	Isabelle Goddard
Highland Heiress	Margaret Moore
Paying the Viking's Price	Michelle Styles
The Highlander's Dangerous Temptation	Terri Brisbin

MEDICAL

The Wife He Never Forgot	Anne Fraser
The Lone Wolf's Craving	Tina Beckett
Sheltered by Her Top-Notch Boss	Joanna Neil
Re-awakening His Shy Nurse	Annie Claydon
A Child to Heal Their Hearts	Dianne Drake
Safe in His Hands	Amy Ruttan

Discover more romance at

www.millsandboon.co.uk

❤ WIN great prizes in our exclusive competitions

❤ BUY new titles before they hit the shops

❤ BROWSE new books and REVIEW your favourites

❤ SAVE on new books with the Mills & Boon® Bookclub™

❤ DISCOVER new authors

PLUS, to chat about your favourite reads, get the latest news and find special offers:

🔲 Find us on facebook.com/millsandboon

🐦 Follow us on twitter.com/millsandboonuk

❤ Sign up to our newsletter at millsandboon.co.uk